A PRINCESS BOUND

A PRINCESS BOUND

NAUGHTY FAIRY TALES FOR WOMEN

EDITED BY
KRISTINA WRIGHT

FOREWORD BY
CATHY YARDLEY

Published in the United States by Cleis Press Inc.,
2246 Sixth Street, Berkeley, California 94710.

Printed in the United States.
Cover design: Scott Idleman/Blink
Cover photograph: Tom Merton/Getty Images
Text design: Frank Wiedemann

First Edition.
10 9 8 7 6 5 4 3 2 1

Trade paper ISBN: 978-1-62778-035-3
E-book ISBN: 978-1-62778-052-0

For Jay,
prince of my heart

Contents

FOREWORD

Cathy Yardley

Once upon a time...

I don't know about you, but when I read those four words, I immediately feel the urge to hunker down in the nearest comfy spot (preferably with a warm beverage) and prepare to give in to an engrossing fantasy.

When you're a child, you know a fairy tale is not going to be mundane. Everything is larger than life: there are dragons, and witches, and curses. Everyone is beautiful, everyone is clever and strong, evil will scare the crap out of you. Whatever else a fairy tale might be, it is never *ordinary.*

But at the heart of every fairy tale, there is also an element of our deepest, most secret hope. "Cinderella" or "Beauty and the Beast," for example, allow us to experience deserving and kind people finally being recognized after a lifetime of being misjudged or overlooked. "Rapunzel" shows an escape from the cage of overprotection. "Sleeping Beauty" illustrates the dream of finding the person who awakens you from a lifetime of stasis and status quo. Fairy tales also allow for vicarious thrill: being taken by a mysterious figure, being held captive—or in the archaic sense, *captivated*—by someone larger than life. Even the villains have a dark, delicious allure.

Fairy tales have gotten a bad rap in recent years. Critics say that they are escape fantasies, teaching people to be passive and hope that a prince, fairy godmother or sheer luck will show up and rescue them.

I don't think that fairy tales teach passivity. Frankly, we have too much activity in our daily lives as it is. We are constantly in situations where we need to act, make decisions and then second-guess ourselves, surrounded by an overabundance of information.

I think that, in a climate where you are constantly faced with the struggles of reality, fairy tales give you a safe environment to experience both your brightest dreams and your darkest desires.

Fairy tales might be cautionary tales or a source of inspiration, but at their heart, they are a *pleasure*, pure and simple.

They don't need to be anything else.

So get your favorite beverage and find a cozy spot to read. We're going to tell you some stories.

Cathy Yardley
Author of *Ravish*

INTRODUCTION: BIND ME, WHIP ME, CALL ME PRINCESS

The original fairy tales were cautionary tales and not for the faint of heart. They warned the reader to stay on the path of righteousness and not stray into the wicked woods, talk to the mysterious stranger or even follow the lure of her dangerous heart lest she face terrible punishment.

A Princess Bound is filled with fairy-tale fantasies that explore the eroticism of BDSM. Here, the princess is not only punished, she is eager for the punishment and the ultimate goal is always exquisite pleasure. Many of the stories in this collection are reimagined versions of the fairy tales you read long ago, some are twisted interpretations of obscure classics and a few are original fairy tales that pay homage to the spirit of myth and legend.

I invite you, dear reader, to bring your own delicious imagination to these erotic tales of dominance and submission. Close the door, loosen the bonds of propriety, let down your hair. Read, enjoy, savor and imagine. *A Princess Bound* will take you where no other fairy-tale collection could—into the most secret of hearts. Your own.

Kristina Wright
Chesapeake, Virginia

SEALED

Laila Blake

James Edward Dowascath gazed fixedly at the shimmering pelt he kept in an iron chest in the attic of his family home on the little spit of land between the icy North Atlantic and the Loch of Swanney on the Orkney mainland. He could hear the wind whistling around the shingles, the sea crashing waves upon waves against the rocks, and his wife singing while she clattered with the dishes. They had always belonged together, like three instruments of a mystical melody: the wailing wind, the sound of the sea and his wife's song.

James was not a weak man; he had the hands of a fisherman: strong and covered in cuts and bruises, in the track marks of rope burn that had dug so deep into his palms and his muscles, he could only fully open his right hand when he pushed it against a flat surface. His neck was sturdy like rope and his shoulders never stooped no matter how heavy the weight he carried. And yet, there were days when that melody was so painful, he thought he might break in two—might take a knife and slice it down his belly and tear out his insides like so many fish entrails. Maybe then his stomach would stop knotting and his chest would stop contracting at the sound. At other times, he called her to him and stroked her white cheekbones with the beautifully huge freckles, more like birthmarks. With a smile, she would drop to her knees, more graciously than any woman he had ever seen, and he would push his hard cock deep into her throat. All that was left was a soft gurgling and the smacking of saliva. No more song.

At other times, he came up here. He unlocked the three heavy locks and pulled out the shimmering pelt. It was like fur and feathers and scales had coalesced into silver and gold, soft and flexible to the touch even after all those years. And like his wife, it had those freckles that contrasted gently with the shimmer. He ran his fingers over the material, shivering a little. It was cool as water even though it wasn't wet and however often he touched it, he could never quite encompass the bizarre sense of the unreal and otherworldly that came upon him like a dousing with cold seawater.

James Edward Dowascath slapped the chest closed with a metallic thud, ignoring his guiltily rapping heart. One after the other, he locked the three locks and then pushed the chest back into the farthest, darkest corner and hid it under blankets and old clothes. He rested only when nothing indicated that he had been there at all, then he rubbed his face, and returned the first key to its place around his neck and the second on a beam under a specific shingle, invisible from below. The third, he took with him downstairs to hide in his workshop in an old jar filled with nails and fishing hooks.

The sealskin was not supposed to exist. It was supposed to be ash and smoke—but James Edward Dowascath, strong and weathered as he was, had never managed to burn it.

* * *

Mairead Dowascath had not always been thus called. James had given her a Christian name the night he'd taken her skin, and then his surname a month later when they were married in the small, crouching Kirkwall Baptist Church an hour's drive from his family home. In the time before her name, she had not needed one and those long seasons had drifted behind a fog bank she could never quite penetrate. Like so many ships avoiding rocky cliffs, she had never dared the perilous journey into the darkness there.

She had no reason: Mairead was happy. She had a loving husband and two children, a boy and a girl, both away at boarding school on the mainland during the week. Her days were spent minding the house and helping her husband when he returned with his daily catch. She enjoyed singing and, when she had the time, she liked to sit on the beach between the rocks and stare out at the endlessly swirling sea. There was a sadness that came over her then, that filled her heart with strength and longing, and she always tumbled back into her husband's arms, eyes gleaming with tears and joy.

She was still beautiful but this distinction had always confused her. She appreciated the glances men especially threw her way and the heat and desire her husband felt for her, but even after many years, she shrugged off compliments, unsure of what to do with them. She was not tall but she possessed a softness of curves, grace and light that was rare in the hardworking community of fishermen and farmers. Her nose was covered in freckles that grew larger on her cheekbones and temples but her skin had never acquired the weathered quality that the salt, the sun and the sea seemed to burn into everybody else. Mairead still shimmered like a fresh-peeled egg, her slowly advancing years visible only in the softest lines around her eyes.

When James came down from the attic and went into his workshop that day, she assumed he'd brought down supplies and was fixing a net or a fish trap. She was preparing a simple dinner, fish soup and fresh bread, and was still humming a melody when he entered the kitchen, looking drawn and tired.

"Are you hungry, my love?" she asked, setting the table.

He came closer; his fingers found her hips and spread around them as he kissed her shoulder.

"Later," he breathed. Mairead recognized the shift in his tone, the heat of his breath, and she leaned against him, her eyes closing. The soup would keep.

Leaning the back of her head onto James's shoulder, she shivered as she felt his fingers undo the twenty-three buttons in the back of her simple dress. With each one, the fabric lay more loosely around her shoulders and started to fall down her arms. James freed it with a final tug, then turned her around. She knew that heat in his glance, the way his eyes wandered down her side to her freckled hip, the softly rounded stomach, and up to her full breasts. It lingered there before he raised his eyes to her lips.

He did not have to speak. Mairead understood each gesture, each glance, and she waited only for the small motion of his middle and index finger to drop to her knees on the rough wooden floor. Her lips stood slightly open the way he had taught her, knees just far enough apart to grant the faintest glimpse at the smooth, glittering folds between her legs. Her eyes were smiling.

There were days when her husband seemed so preoccupied, so drawn and sad, she all but pleaded with him to let her serve him, just to rub his feet or rub and kiss his back until the smile was back in his face. At others, he caught her by surprise with the heat and desperation of his need for her.

Mairead had never wondered what other married folk did in the privacy of their bedroom, could not remember parents, priests or teenage friends who could have given her any frame of reference of right and wrong. James was her reference—and ever since they met, their love had run hotter and darker than anything she had ever known. She craved his touch—the hard ones just as much as the gentle ones, with every fiber of her soul, even now, after years and years together.

Kneeling on that floor, the grain of the wood biting into the skin of her knees, she looked up at him with longing as he reached for a stretch of rope and looped it around her neck, hair and all, before proceeding to drag her toward their small bedroom. It left Mairead grappling, struggling on all fours not to stay too far behind lest the rope cut into her neck. And yet, inevitably, it always did and then she wanted to whimper and press her fingers hard between her legs.

When James Edward Dowascath met his future wife for the first time, he was a young lad of nineteen years, strong and full of dreams and desires. When he met her again, seven years later, the years of waiting and thinking of his one true love had turned him prematurely grim and solitary.

The first time, it was by chance. He had spent a long day at a cousin's wedding in Kirkwall—a loud event with too many people, and his aunts pushing him toward young women who all laughed too loudly at the boys who were fool enough to make advances while the girls were in packs. He'd found himself by the sea that evening, letting the sound of the waves wash his ear canals clean. And there she was, naked and bathing in the ocean, scattering the moonlight about herself like liquid silver. He had called to her and she had smiled—that beautiful, innocent smile that she still had. They had made love on the wet sand in the surf, where he had made her kneel on all fours. Afterward they had cleaned themselves together and she had lain in his arms and she had begged him not to let her go. But James had not understood, had smiled and promised without knowing what she'd meant. He was not a man who believed in fairy tales and old myths.

The next morning, he woke up to the high tide licking at his feet and the girl was gone. He waited for her for weeks, night after night but she never came back and James grew bitter and lonely as the seasons passed.

Seven years later, he was a different man. He owned the family house and lived alone, a fisherman who nobody had called "young man" in years. His lined and dour face seemed to suggest a man far older than his twenty-six years. And one night, another full moon, he was awakened by a rap at the door.

There she was, his girl. Unlike him, she had not changed, not at all, she was still naked and soft and she still shimmered in the moonlight. Her eyes met his and her hand, still cold and wet, ran over his saddened, aged features as though she could wash the years away.

"Why did you let me go?" she asked. And that night, he tied her to his bed and he made her scream and writhe and beg and whimper like he had never seen a woman before, in pleasure he hadn't known was possible. In the morning, her wrists and ankles had been red with rope burn and she'd told him what to do: how to find her skin and how to burn it so that the pull of the ocean could not draw her away from him like the tide.

He had found the pelt hidden between the rocks at the beach, had felt the same eerie sense of the inhuman power that still made him shiver and he had hidden it away. Somehow to put it to the torch would have been like pushing his beautiful girl's face into the fire and he could not bear it. Not for all these years of doubt when he saw her eyes lost on the infinite ocean, longing for something she did not remember and which he could not comprehend.

The rope had remained, and her slippery body that had given them both so much pleasure over the years.

"Up," James breathed hoarsely and watched Mairead climb onto their hard, narrow bed. Her round buttocks raised high in the air, she looked back at him over her freckled shoulder. The rope was taut between them and her eyes shone like the stars reflecting on the dark, still ocean.

It was the rope, always the rope when his hold on her felt as tentative, as fleeting as it did that day. James wrapped it once around it his hand and it lay easily in the old, scarred groove across his palm. It forced Mairead's back into a round, deep hollow, bending her head back as she gulped down audible breaths, forcing the oxygen past the obstruction against her neck. It was a spectacle James had always loved to watch, not least because Mairead seemed unable not to roll her hips, furtively and futilely trying to find something to rub her cunt against.

This time, James found the loose end of the rope, coiled it once until it had formed a small, hard loop and rubbed it against her slippery wet places where his strange and beautiful wife had never once sprouted body hair like regular humans. It was hard and rough hemp rope, nothing like the relative smoothness of his hands and fingers—let alone the velvety quality of his cock. And yet, Mairead could have dissolved in sudden gratitude. He rubbed it along her slit and up to the little nub at the top. Too tender for such treatment, she flinched away only to regret the lack of contact immediately and bear back down against the offered surface.

James smiled. He had always loved to watch her, to play with her while his organ grew painfully hard in his trousers and only take her once she was sweaty and all but delirious with desire. She was stunning when she yielded like this, no self-conscious or worrying bone in her body, but James loathed losing control himself. His was a different pleasure.

He found himself watching her most tender skin grow red and raw in places—such a beautiful coloring. He shivered, squared his jaw and then pulled the rope away, subconsciously measuring its length. Mairead whimpered in protest, her ass humping the air until James gave in and slapped it, hard, once or twice. Only then, Mairead let her head hang, catching her breath while the sting of pain slowly dissolved in heat waves over her rear. She was his beautiful, impossible creature: a woman, not reared to live in shame.

James let her calm down for a minute or so, watched her thighs quiver and cunt contract against air a few times—such a hungry, greedy little thing. He resisted the urge to give it something to contract around. Not yet.

Looping the rope between her legs and down under her body, he rested his knee on the bed and pulled the rope tight. Mairead moaned, her head pulled back once more.

"Open," he commanded as he brought the end of the rope, coarse and dirty and smelling of cunt and sea, to her lips. When she obeyed as she always did, he pushed it in her mouth and ordered her to bite down hard. She was gasping for air, chasing the friction the rope could offer, when she managed to drag it up against her slit and James sat back to watch.

"Harder," he breathed once and his hand found his shaft as he saw her repeatedly choking herself just to feel that bit of coarse rope rub up and down her cunt and the crack of her ass—was it just because he'd told her to?

It was quite a while until he got up—not before he could see the reddened flesh between the round cheeks, not before her face had lost some of its color. He took the rope from between her teeth, then loosened it around her neck without actually taking it off. Mairead was breathing heavily, rubbing her face against his shirt while he petted her hair.

"What a beautiful, perfect woman you are," he whispered and she beamed at him as she always did. He smiled back at her, cradled her face and brushed his thumbs over her freckled cheekbones. With a pang of guilt, a stab in his gut, the tactile memory of brushing over the freckles on her pelt entered his mind. His eyes dilated only momentarily and then he pushed her down until her sweet mouth enveloped his cock and he could lean his head back in exquisite pleasure that might drive the pain away.

He pushed deep, deep to find the gurgling, the rhythmic contractions of her throat as it tried to rid itself from the obstruction that, too, hindered her breathing. It brought tears to her eyes, and he smeared them over her cheekbones until they glinted in the oil lamp that illuminated the room. When he came with a sudden groan, more that of a hurt animal than a man, she drank down his offering with shining eyes and James leaned onto the bed, dropping next to where she still knelt. Mairead kissed his shoulder and his arm, but he was not happy. He had lost control too fast, and unlike his wife who never seemed to tire, he was a not a young man anymore who could recuperate in a matter of minutes. He did not apologize; Mairead did not expect him to—she looked, in fact, more satisfied by the exchange than James, whose brow was furrowed as he drew her against his chest, lying on their narrow cot.

Touching his lips, then his cleft chin, Mairead smiled up at her husband, caressed him with those fingers that could never lie still when they were close enough to touch him. His eyes closed and he relaxed slowly as her lips fluttered down his neck.

"The band is running thin, do you want me to find a new one?" she asked and James blinked. Had he fallen asleep, maybe just for a minute? He looked at where her gaze hung at the leather band around his neck and he flushed with a guilty sense of dizziness. Quickly, he pushed the key back under his shirt and managed a smile.

"Don't worry about it my dear, I'll see to it tomorrow."

Mairead didn't question him; she kissed his lips and they rested a while longer until she served his dinner. The soup was still warm, the bread still fresh. And maybe, just maybe he could gather his strength and try again after a meal. In his head, he had the vivid image of holding the end of the rope like a horse's reins and pulling her kneeling figure back onto his cock with each stroke. He felt it harden into life to these images, watching her carefully scooping soup onto the same tongue that had minutes before tasted his come.

It was the first week in May and although still cold, the sun had shown its face over the water more steadily than it had in months. With James out with his boat and his crew, Mairead had scrubbed the house and prepared the evening meal. She had planned to spend the rest of the day sewing—it was almost time for the summer holidays and she relished the thought of having her children about her day by day. There was a ceremony at the end of term that they would attend, fetching them home afterward, and Mairead needed a dress for the occasion. She was an economic woman and before traveling into town for new fabric, she went into the attic to see what she might rescue from old pieces. She did not like the attic, the way she had to stoop with every step, but she also wanted to look over the children's holiday clothes, the things they could wear at home when the school uniform would be left in the wardrobe for weeks and they could get dirty like children should.

She was kneeling on the dusty ground, several piles of clothes arranged around her when she spied another heap in the corner. Not for the first time that afternoon, she slammed her head against a beam when she went to investigate. Holding her aching forehead, she looked up. A little dust was falling down on her face amid a leather band. It hung in the air, impossibly defying gravity.

Mairead pulled. There was the sound of metal scraping softly over wood, and then a key fell into her hand. A key like the one around James's neck. A band like the one that had worn thin. She didn't know why but she slipped it into a pocket of her dress with a dizzying sense of wrongdoing. It was when she found the chest under the pile of clothes that she knew why. Three locks. Two keys. With shaking hands, she tried the first one, almost relieved it didn't fit. But the second sprung open almost as though it had been oiled the day before.

Mairead shivered, immediately deciding to forget about the chest and the keys. She went back downstairs, then down to the sea, but the beach only seemed to intensify the heady sensation that a dark fog was fast approaching, ready to swallow her whole.

She dashed back into the house, fueled by curiosity almost against her will and she cried when she found James's key in his workshop; there between nets that needed mending was the band that had finally snapped where it had run thin. She clutched it to her chest and then searched for the last. In a way, she knew it was wrong, that she shouldn't—but what in the world could James keep so terrifyingly secret? And why?

Back on her knees in front of the chest hours before she

expected James to return, she opened the remaining locks. Tears came to her eyes even before she saw the shimmering pelt. There it rested, like liquid silver and a torrent of memories washed over her like a sudden tide, a dousing tsunami that dragged her back into the sea, struggling and fighting hand and foot. But the ocean had no mercy and it was too late for an appeal—it was recalling its daughter like a debt that had never been repaid.

In the years that followed, James never saw his wife again, however often he looked for her when the full moon was high in the sky. Sometimes, he saw his children playing in the surf with a band of seals—and then they would laugh and jump with joy and James would watch them from his window, tears running down his cheeks. He would wait for the next full moon, and sit between the rocks year after year, while his bones grew brittle and his skin like paper around them. He watched his son take over the house and the business, a fisherman like no other, with a sixth sense for finding the largest swarms and a mysterious glint in his eyes that made the village girls swoon. He watched his daughter grow slowly into the same quiet and graceful beauty that her mother had been, too good for any man who asked for her hand even when she fell in love and James gave his blessing only grudgingly.

And still he waited between the rocks, until she came for him one cold night in November. She stepped out of the sea, peeling herself from her skin, naked and perfect. Then she kissed him and took him back with her into the cold, crashing waves.

IN THE PALACE OF GODS AND MONSTERS

Michelle Augello-Page

Long ago, in a forgotten time, a princess awoke, startled by ink-black darkness, grasping for where she was. She was blindfolded. She was naked. She couldn't move; her arms and legs were stretched out, bound tightly with rope to wooden posts. She pulled and twisted her body, but her movement caused the ropes to pull painfully on her wrists and ankles. She cried out, and an unfamiliar voice, dark and honeyed, filled the room.

"You truly are beautiful, princess."

She struggled again, fear rushing through her, as the full weight of her situation grew clearer in her mind. "Be still, my bride," he said, hushing her as he advanced toward the bed. "I have come to welcome you. I am not going to harm you."

His hand traced the outline of her body, and she shuddered at the whisper of his touch. The princess cried, barely able to process what was happening. Just that morning, she had awakened in her own bed, in her own home, safe and happy and cared for. Now, she was held like a prisoner by a man who assumed himself to be her husband.

Her family had fallen in nobility and depended upon her marriage to restore their fortune. From birth, the princess was educated accordingly and trained to be the wife of the finest king. Tales of the princess's beauty had spread far and wide, and she was shielded from the world, sheltered in a remote castle tucked into the craggy cliffs overlooking the sea. Those who braved the journey were rewarded by her otherworldly beauty and graciousness, but the princess had kindly rejected all offers of marriage.

"I will recognize my love when I see his face," she had insisted.

Her fate changed when the messenger came to the castle. He brought an offer from the king of a faraway palace, and enough riches and jewels to reclaim the fullness of the family's royalty. Her mother and father were desperate. They tried to persuade her. They tried to reason with her. But the princess had been raised on fairy tales; she believed in love. The offer stood until the sun went down. There was nothing to pack, nothing to bring; the messenger said that the master of the kingdom would provide all and more for the princess. The king and queen could not, would not, allow her to refuse.

Her dreams shattered, the princess was betrothed, sight unseen. Her mother and father had thrown her into the carriage, ignoring her pleas, and forced her into the marriage in exchange for all the wealth they had hoped she would bring.

"You have had a long journey. I understand you need a little time to acclimate to your new role. I am not a monster." He cleared his throat, and continued. "But I am no ordinary man either, and there are rules to be followed, now that you belong to me."

He circled the bed, never taking his eyes off her, and even blindfolded, she could feel his eyes upon her nakedness, drinking in the curves of her soft, pale skin and the pinkness of her nipples. She blushed, thinking of her legs spread and the agonizing breeze that teased the tender place between her thighs.

"In the daylight, you are free to go anywhere you please in the palace, as well as anywhere in the valley. You will find everything you may desire here. Being from such a remote place yourself, I doubt you will be offended by the lack of population. During the day, you will be alone."

She could hear him walking around her, the air whooshing slightly as he walked, the sound reminiscent of the rustle of feathers. The princess listened to the deep tone of his sensual voice; the rise and fall of his cadence soothed her, and almost against her will, she felt herself calming.

"When the darkness falls, you will get ready for me. You will extinguish all lights, and prepare yourself with a blindfold. Then, and only then, I will come to you, and I will train you as my wife."

He cleared his throat again.

"You may never touch me. You may never see me."

The princess gasped.

"That is all."

Alone and uncomfortable in the desperate quiet, she wept. She cried herself to sleep, and when she awoke again in the morning, the ropes had disappeared, and she was free, free in the strange hold of her new environment. She reluctantly explored the palace, half fearing what would happen when the sun went down, half hoping it had all been a dream.

Throughout the palace, carvings of gods and monsters were depicted in the marble accenting each room. She was unable to suppress her delight in the surprise each room held—exquisite works of art, the finest musical instruments, a studio overlooking the lush, bright green valley, shelved with leather-bound books—and she thought she might be happy there, after all.

By nightfall, the princess had resigned herself to fate. All light had been extinguished, and she sat on the edge of the bed in a dress and blindfold. She lay down and restlessly waited for what seemed like hours, until that same slight rustle of movement alerted her that he had arrived.

The princess's heart beat furiously.

Silently, he stood above her and felt her face. Strong hands re-secured the cloth blinding her sight. He moved quickly, telling her to put her hands above her head, then used the rope to tie her wrists together. He stripped her, pulling the dress roughly over her head and arms, then spread her legs, tying each foot to a post, leaving her naked and exposed.

"This is how I want you," he said.

Light kisses fluttered across the surface of her skin, arousing her, brushing against her, tickling her with wisps of feathery touch, heightening her desire. He pinned her wrists above her head and kissed her full on the mouth until she kissed him back, tentatively at first, then passionately, hungrily, lips and teeth and tongue.

Sensation rippled through her as his other hand pulled on her pink nipples until she cried out. He moved lower, finding her honey spot wet and hot with desire. Gently, slowly, he rubbed against her slickness with deliberate softness, gingerly working her breath into a hum, breaking her resistance into ragged cries for more.

"Do you like that, princess?"

"Yes," she moaned, as he stretched her arms farther above her head and tied her to the bed frame.

Waves of pleasure washed over her consciousness, leaving her body uninhibited and wanting. Still, she screamed and shuddered when his rock-hard cock entered her sharply and tore into her ruthlessly. Still, she cried as he took her completely, claiming her as his.

The next morning, she awoke unbound and alone, but the imprint of his touch lingered everywhere on her skin.

Day turned to night, and night to day, and so the time passed, and the princess grew to love her husband. He told her he loved her in a million different ways, but still, she did not see his face. And though she loved and desired him, the feelings he aroused in her scared her. His power over her scared her.

He touched her with the wings of an angel. He growled as ferociously as a beast. She wondered if the lashes she felt, bitter and scorching, tearing across her skin, were the claws of a monster or the tools of a man. He brought her so far into the realm of the gods, that she was no longer herself; she was a body releasing soul, universal and unconscious, pure energy, primal and sexual and spiritual, cosmic, one with all.

She had changed. Her body had become a sexually charged light field, blooming recklessly with dark desires. He took her to both heaven and hell. He took her so far into the depths of pleasure and pain that she did not know if he was human, monster or god.

Each night, she submitted to his enchantment, bound and stretched, cursed and blessed. Each night, she was pulled apart and put together again. And she faced her darkness in the glaring light of day, alone.

She had to see his face. She had to see him.

The thought obsessed her until one night, she gathered the courage to ask her husband to untie her before she slept. She told him that her body was sore, that she needed rest. He hesitated, then reasoned that he had been hard on the princess that evening, and she had taken his rough love wholly and completely, as always.

He decided to grant her request.

But the princess held that deceit in her heart, and waited until she heard her husband's breath deepen into telltale sleep. Then she crept quietly from the bed and across the room, each shifting of the floorboards stilling her with fear. But her husband slept on, and she continued on, out of the room in search of a candle.

She cupped the light between her hands until it was a sliver between her glowing fingers. Her heart beat loudly and her breath quickened as she advanced, allowing the light to fall across the bed. Above him she stood, stock-still, barely able to believe the vision before her.

His beauty was beyond compare. His perfect arms and legs and torso gleamed in the golden light like chiseled marble. Lying across the bed, he looked like a fallen god, sensual and beautiful and cruel. Shimmering dark hair fell across his shoulders, revealing the profile of his face. She moved closer.

He stirred, and the princess started. A drop of wax fell on her sleeping husband, and he awoke.

The quiet calm of his sleeping, cherubic beauty quickly shattered, as he realized what was happening. The princess blew out the candle, but too late, and his anger roared throughout the palace and over the valley.

"How could you betray me?"

"I just wanted to see—"

"You have destroyed us."

Angrily he walked across the room, his human form changing, morphing, shaping the muscles in his back. Feathers fell to the ground as his wings grew stronger, and he flexed and stretched anxiously as he continued his path forward until he reached the window and shattered the glass violently, flying through the window, shards of glass and broken feathers flying, flying away.

"What have I done?" The princess sunk to the ground in despair.

He did not come the next night, nor did he come the night after that. She waited anxiously for him each night, her heart growing heavier as the hours grew long, and woke each morning wrecked, abandoned and alone. She did not know if she would ever see him again. She did not know what would become of her.

On the third night, as she had each night since he left, she removed her clothing and attached the blindfold to her eyes. She waited, desperately wanting to believe that he would return, and her heart jumped when she heard him enter the room.

"You were never supposed to see me. You agreed to the terms. You betrayed me. This absolves my marriage to you."

He unfastened the cloth blinding her vision.

"No," she protested.

"Have you seen me?"

She shook her head, and tried to cover her face. He stopped her, grabbing her arms and holding her wrists hard.

"Look at me."

"Please," she pleaded, resisting him at first. She was afraid of what she would see. But he held her wrists until she could no longer bear it. Pain. Anger. Love.

"I am sorry."

"You betrayed my trust."

"Please, understand how I needed to see you. I needed to see the face of the one I love. Don't you see how you have changed me? What you have given to me? I was scared. I didn't know who you are, what you are. I love you. I needed to see you. How could I believe in you, when you hid your face from me? How could I trust in what I could not see? But I was wrong. I didn't know that I had already seen you with my eyes blindfolded. I didn't realize that I had seen you a million times in my dreams."

The hard resolve of his heart softened, as he saw the purity of her love laid bare.

"We see with our souls, not our eyes."

"Yes," the princess said.

"You will be punished."

He reached out his hand to her, and she took it. "And if you can endure my torments, and if you can learn your lessons, then we will live openly in the palace of gods and monsters, in view of all that is mortal and immortal, and you will be changed forever."

The princess nodded.

"Follow me."

She followed him outside, into the garden, the night blooming wildly with the perfume of honeysuckle and moonflower. Under the stars, he bound her ankles with rope, and then threw the rope across a heavy tree limb. He told her to lie down on the bare earth, and she did, skin brushing grass and dirt, pressing against the uneven and exposed roots. He hoisted her up, up, upside down, and she fell toward the sky. Blood rushed to her head, flushing her face and neck red. The world changed and her sense of balance shifted; she swayed nervously, afraid, as he secured the rope. She was suspended as precariously as the hanged man, her face level with his cock.

Hard and aggressive, he was magnificently erect and stood before the princess bound, swinging upside down, her long hair brushing the earth. All she could see was his thrusting phallus as he grabbed her hips and swung her forward, pushing his cock into her mouth, deep into her throat, sliding in and out of her lips as she struggled to contain him; again and again, she opened for him, her mouth hot and wet and wanting.

He withdrew quickly and, holding his swollen cock like a loaded gun, shot his ejaculation across the princess's body, releasing his seed across the landscape of her skin.

Slowly, he released the princess from her bondage, lowering her closer to the ground, altering her sense of gravity again as he returned her to earth. Several drops of semen had fallen upon the grass. He pointed to the seed, glowing white in the moonlight; and she knelt, licking the blades clean.

He returned again the next night.

Again, she had placed a blindfold over her eyes. Again, he untied it, forcing the princess to look upon his form.

He shone as if the surface of his skin was lit from within.

Around her neck, he placed a collar, affixed with a leash. He tugged on the leash, and she obeyed, falling to all fours. Grabbing her hair, he pulled her face higher, forcing her to position proudly. She took a deep breath when he let go, and walked around her to admire her form. Then, he pulled her to standing and, holding on to the leash, led her outside, out of the garden and into the meadow, where the sheep spent their days grazing. He tied her to a post, and she knelt on the earth again, dirt kissing the palms of her hands and small pebbles biting her knees.

He left her tied, captive, as if she were common as a wayward sheep. She waited and waited under the starry sky, trying to remember the names of the constellations, trying to forget all thought of past or future. She was born a princess bound to fate. She was the wind against her skin, the vastness of the bright night sky. Her eyes still held the sun-kissed sparkle of the faraway sea.

The meadow was enclosed with low, thorny bushes, and he returned holding a switch. Golden fleece had caught in the thorns of the branch. He ran the switch along the princess's back, and she twitched with laughter, feeling the scratch and soft bristle along her spine. He rubbed the branch against her ass, teasing her lightly, then attacking her roughly, making her roar with laughter, then slowly moving down her legs to her feet, pulling the fleece between her toes, tickling her mercilessly.

He handed the switch to the princess. “Remove the fleece.”

Nimbly releasing the golden thread from the thorny branch, the princess handed him back the switch and gave him the fleece, then resumed her position.

Pain seared across her ass as he hit her with the switch, the thorns scratching her tender skin in thin, cruel lines. She cried out, wincing, and he soothed her, rubbing the burn with the soft cloud of fleece, then tortured her more with what seemed like a thousand fingers light as feathers until her laughter floated throughout the valley and released a chorus of echoes across the star-shattered sky.

On the third night, the princess did not affix the blindfold, as he had removed it the previous two nights. She waited for him nervously in the darkness, not knowing for sure whether or not he would come, and if he did come, what kind of punishment she was to receive. A dark thrill surged throughout her body as she waited, wanting, her heart beating wildly with both fear and desire.

When he arrived, he felt her face, and found it unbound by the cloth.

“Bring the light here,” he said, and she lit a candle, illuminating the room with soft light and dancing shadows.

“You are not done with your punishment.”

“I understand,” the princess answered him, averting her eyes.

“I don’t want you to take your eyes off me.”

The princess nodded, and peered into his black depths.

He worked quickly, and she watched him, his beautiful,

perfect body glimmering, obscenely shifting in the shadows, bulging with fat and fur. On the floor, she struggled for balance, bound with rope, wrists and ankles tied, and tied again, contorting her body into an arc, a bow. Losing and gaining her center of gravity, she stumbled, afraid.

She watched him as he silently, slowly circled her. Light and shadow crossed his hideous face as he disciplined her. The princess cried as the whip cracked against her tender skin. Rush of air. Sharp pain. Stinging pain. He placed a basin under her face as she rocked helplessly, hog-tied on the floor.

"Tonight, you will fill this with your tears."

She strained, feeling the pain in the stretch of her body and the furious touch of the whip against her skin. She watched him through her tears, seeing the cruelness in his sensual mouth as he struck her, his features hard and fearsome, his flesh crawling across his cage of bone, morphing grotesquely in the soft flickering light. She cried, thinking of how her mother and father had thrown her away and flung her into the world alone and unprepared, abandoning her to fate. She cried, thinking about how she had changed, how she was once a simple child, thinking the world all magic and mystery, not yet knowing pain or cruelty or fear. The lashes struck her paper-thin, tender skin over and again, and she wept openly. He was a monster. His face was distorted, and he moved inhumanly in the candlelit shadows. She cried and cried, releasing a river of tears, enough to drown in.

When he was done, she watched him spill the contents of the basin into a goblet. He raised the glass to his lips and they looked at each other for a moment before he drank it down, tilting his head back so that he could receive it all in one swallow. She looked at him as if looking into a mirror; his eyes were her eyes, her pain was his pain.

In the morning, she awoke with his arms around her, the full brightness of the morning star flooding the room. His lips were half open, pursed in half-sleep twilight, lost in waking dreams. She touched his rough cheek, then kissed the curve of his neck, breathing him in. He stirred as she looked upon his face.

He opened his eyes, and kissed each of hers, licking the tears from each lash. Then he found her lips and kissed her passionately, searching her mouth with his own. His tongue slipped between her soft lips, sending thrills of desire and deep want inside her. He touched her breasts, lightly teasing her nipples, then harder, twisting and licking and biting until she moaned. He moved on top of her, pressing the weight of his body against her body. She touched his shoulders, then ran her hands across his strong back, feeling the length of his spine. She grabbed his supple ass, digging her fingers into his flesh, and his long thick cock caressed her, pressing against her cunt.

He fell into her, eye to eye, as his throbbing cock entered her, moving slowly and deliberately inside her, then faster, rougher, as he thrust deeper. Arms and legs contorted in esoteric positions, suspended pleasure-pain, searching the surface of skin for the key to the soul. He rocked her into a state of rapture, sliding in and out of her pussy, expanding inside her, exploding inside her, breaking her cries into growls and moans, then taking her farther, fucking her harder, consuming her, releasing her, freeing her.

They were breaking together, spinning and spiraling, bringing each other higher and higher, transcending consciousness, being/nonbeing, losing awareness of both mind and body, existing in fragments of air and pieces of sky. Their combined energy pushed into the ecstatic, releasing them into the unknown. They fell into nothingness, into the wordless, soundless sea of the cosmos, and for a brief, blissful moment, they were cradled in the universal womb, the place before life and after death, the place of dreams and transformation, the place where all is born again, anew.

He kissed her tenderly as she cried, keeping her close in his tight embrace, encircling her with his body, enfolding her with fierce, protective love. And each night, and each day thereafter, they awoke together, bound happily in pain and pleasure, in the palace of gods and monsters, part of the world's dream.

THE DANCING PRINCESS

Elizabeth L. Brooks

You've heard the story, no doubt, of my sisters and me, and how our father was vexed by the state of our shoes. How a common soldier managed to outwit us all and bring back to our father proof of the Realm where we danced each night. And how Father gave me to this soldier as a reward.

The story ends there, blithely "happily-ever-after." No one ever asked me how I felt about it.

I don't know what I would have said if I had been asked, though, so perhaps that's fair. I was in shock for days. That I was to be wed to a man I did not know was nothing; I had always been destined for a stranger: to seal a treaty, to serve as hostage, to strengthen an alliance. Such is the fate of a nobleman's daughter. But that Father would give me to a commoner—no matter how clever!

At least the soldier was young and handsome and whole, apart from a slight limp, unlike the Archduke, to whom my eldest sister has been betrothed for over a decade. (I never questioned *her* need to sneak out of the palace and lose herself in frivolity while she still could.)

Unlike my sister, I was not to be allowed the comfort of a long betrothal. I was still half-stunned when, a mere ten days later, I was married. My chemise was shot with silver thread and the overdress cut from cloth-of-gold; as the servants stitched me into it, I wondered who had ordered it. Its beauty taunted me with reminders of the enchanted forest of the Realm, which I would never see again.

Numbly, I let them lead me through the rituals and pageantry; I waved and smiled at the thronging crowd, I followed meekly to the church, I repeated my vows for the priest, I sipped from the cup of wine.

It wasn't until the priest pronounced us husband and wife that I began to awaken. My new husband took me in his arms and I steeled myself for the touch of his lips. It was no chaste kiss he gave me, there on the steps of the altar. Soldier that he was, he thrust his tongue into my mouth like a battering ram, and before I could begin to understand this intrusion, it was gone and instead his teeth closed on my lower lip hard enough that I squeaked with surprise and the beginning of fear. When he released me, the look he gave me was possessive and dark, perhaps even cruel. My innards fluttered and shuddered at that look.

The feast was a blur. My husband's eyes were on me constantly (did he think I would try to flee? I had more dignity than that) but he spoke to me only once, to introduce an old woman of his acquaintance. She patted my hand, cackled wordlessly and nodded to him as if sealing some marketplace bargain.

Despite the limp in his wounded leg, my soldier led me through the dance well enough. If he was lacking in the smooth gentility of the courtiers who had taught me or the hectic joy of my lost partners of the Realm, I must admit there was something in the coarse grip of his hands at my waist that offered up a dim echo of the excitement I'd once felt, following in my sisters' wakes as we hurried toward our pleasures.

Eventually, the festivities were done, and we were shut into the bridal suite for the consummation, the moment I had been dreading. Clever he might be, but he was a soldier, a brute. My lip still stung from the kiss with which he had wed me; I did not dare contemplate what sort of assault he would mount on my other, more tender parts.

He did not, as I half expected, immediately throw himself upon me and begin ripping at my clothes. He merely stood, looking at me. I did not know what to do. Did he expect me to act like a camp follower, flinging myself upon him and regaling him with coarse, lewd suggestion? Even had that been my desire or inclination, I could not: I knew nothing of such things. For all my schooling, of the mysteries of the marital bed I had been taught only to await my future husband's teaching. I waited, watching him as he watched me, until I was so overcome with my own doubt and ignorance that I was forced to drop my gaze. I fidgeted with my fingers, and finally spoke out of a desperate need to fill this terrible silence.

"Won't you sit, my lord? Your leg must pain you—"

"I am not a lord," he interrupted, "as I think you well know."

"Of course. Forgive me," I said. "Will you sit?"

"I am comfortable enough." He stepped closer, then, and closer still, until I could feel the heat of his body, but I did not quite dare to look up into his face. "You are very beautiful," he said softly.

Such a simple statement, stripped bare of the embellishments and false humility I was accustomed to receiving from the courtiers. I wondered briefly if this simplicity was how common folk wooed. Then I remembered that we were wed, and he had no need for wooing. He would touch me now with his rough hands, I thought, perhaps bruise my tender flesh. I thought of his subterfuge in the Realm, where he had whipped my shoulders with his stolen branches from the enchanted forest, and was surprised by a sudden spread of warmth in my belly.

If his hands were coarse, they were more gentle than I had expected as he unlaced the overdress and lifted its gem-encrusted weight off my shoulders. The silver-shot chemise beneath was sewn on, meant to be ripped free, but my husband did not take hold of the fabric. Instead, he stepped back, merely looking at me once again.

I hazarded a glance at his face and found his eyes on mine immediately, as if he had been waiting for just such a moment. His gaze was dark and fierce; I was put in mind of a painting I had seen once of a wolf standing guard over his chosen prey. The warmth in my belly swelled, and I caught my breath in surprise.

He smiled at that, a secretive and knowing smile that made my limbs quiver. I fought to maintain my dignity, casting my thoughts for any topic of conversation that might bring him back to the grave but courteous bridegroom he had been during our wedding feast. His hand was rising; I could not predict its course, but knew that I must—must!—stave off his touch, or be, somehow, lost.

Panic scattered my wits and poise to the winds, and I blurted the first words that came to mind. "Why me?"

His hand halted in its course, paused and fell. His eyebrows raised, questioning, and I pressed onward, my heart racing like a hunted rabbit's. "Why not one of my elder sisters? You might have been prince-consort!"

That knowing smile lingered on his lips, and he shook his head. "I do not want to be a prince," he said softly, "or a duke, or an earl. I wanted..." Caught in his gaze, I had not noticed his hand moving again; he captured my hand and lifted it to his lips. Recalling the kiss with which we had been wed, I shivered at his touch and barely suppressed a whimper of fear. But the brush of his lips over my knuckles was as soft as a rose petal, and I flushed in relief.

He drew nearer still, until I could feel his breath ghosting across the bare skin of my neck. "I wanted you."

"But why?" I asked, begging like a lost child. "Why me?"

Any bridegroom with half a heart would spin a tale of pretty words at such a question, invent some infatuation with her beauty or charm to set his frightened maiden-wife at ease. My husband did no such thing. He touched my face with his calloused fingertips, then put his lips to my ear and said, "Because, my lovely one, I was watching in the silver forest, when I used the branches to whip your shoulders, and in the golden forest, when I used the branches to flog your thighs, and I saw your reaction."

The heat in my belly became a fire, spreading down into my sex. I feared it, as I feared him, and I stepped back, seeking to flee, even as my sisters and I had when we had discovered our Realm's sanctity violated. "What reaction?" I demanded. "I cried out, as my sisters did, in pain!"

But I was not allowed to retreat. My husband's arm caught me about the waist, as if we were dancing, and spun me into an even closer embrace. "Not all cries are the same," he murmured, and smiled down into my face, the heat in his predator's eyes burning through me, possessing me.

What was this fire in my body, and why did it leap and spark at the terrible hunger in his gaze? "I don't understand,"

I moaned helplessly. My limbs were trembling. "Please, you're frightening me!"

"Am I?" he asked. His tongue traced the shell of my ear, delicate as a butterfly's wing. His arms were strong, his body warm and hard. I melted into the caress with a sigh, let my body fall against his, felt his member, full and hot against my belly as if there were no clothes between us—and then he bit down, sharp and quick, on my earlobe. Half a shriek escaped before I clenched my teeth and turned the sound into a whimper.

"You're hurting me!" I protested, though in truth he had already returned to gentle kisses, nuzzling at my neck and jaw.

"Shall I stop?" he asked. Matching deed to word, he pushed sharply and I found myself at his arm's length, no part of him touching me. Only the hot challenge in his eyes remained of the warmth in which he had folded me, and I felt suddenly, inexplicably, bereft.

Unbidden by any conscious desire, I swayed toward him. "No," I whispered, though it made my skin prickle and flush to admit it. "Don't stop."

He held out his arms, and this time I went willingly into them, shivering with as much need as fear when they enfolded me. He gathered me close, letting me feel the heat and hardness of his body again. "My lovely princess," he whispered, covering my face with the most tender of kisses.

His hand was between us, then, reaching into his jacket (for a mad moment, I wondered at his callousness, to interrupt this moment to check his pocket watch) and then I saw what was in his hand. He uncoiled a short quirt, nearly small enough to be a child's toy, braided from the silver and gold branches of the trees of the Realm, the dangling strands springy and flexible. If his arm had not been around me, holding me up, I might have fallen then, for my knees grew weak with fear even as the fire in my loins began to rage.

"How do you imagine it will feel?" my husband asked, his voice full of warmth and delight. His eyes were on my face again, I knew, though I could not tear my gaze from the little whip. He lifted it and let the ends trail coolly across the skin above my décolletage. I shuddered, though I could not have said whether it was in fear or desire. Indeed, even more than the quirt itself, I feared my reaction to it.

My husband led me to the waiting bed, and I let him arrange me on it to his satisfaction, though I blushed so hard my cheeks ached. He bent me over its edge like a naughty child over a governess's knee, and raised the silver-shot cloth over my hips, exposing my thighs and buttocks to the open air. He caressed the exposed skin while I squirmed, whimpering with I knew not what desperate need, and when he slipped a finger between my thighs and into my passage, I sobbed aloud.

He withdrew, and for an instant I wondered if he had finished with me so quickly—but then I heard the soft whistle and felt the first shocking sting of the whip against my skin, just at the fold where cheek curves into leg. I yelped, but the pain lasted only for a moment and then transmuted into a fiery burn that radiated out from the line of impact. It seemed to both ease and feed the fire inside me. I groaned.

My husband chuckled. "Yes, my lovely one," he breathed. "I knew you would feel it properly." He stooped close and kissed the welt, and I writhed and whimpered, needing both cessation and continuation. I didn't even hear the whistle this time before the quirt struck again, on my other side. I keened through the pain, but when it had again transformed, my greedy hips waggled, begging for more.

My husband laughed again, a hint of growl altering his voice.

"You dance delightfully," he said, and struck again.

And again. And again, until even the initial pain of his strokes became no more than fingers of the fire that was consuming me, inside and out.

When, finally, he dropped the whip, I was sobbing, not for him to stop, but for the fire to finally complete its work and engulf me entirely. He lifted me the rest of the way onto the bed and turned me onto my back. The welts on my buttocks and thighs made even the fine silk sheets feel as coarse and rough as straw under my skin, and my husband smiled with precious cruelty at my whimpers and squirming.

His strong, soldier's hands finally tore away the gown and he stretched out against me and I wondered, but only briefly, when he had taken off his clothes. His manhood, pressing against my hip, was full and thick, and I felt drawn to it like a magnet. I rolled toward him, and he pressed me back, enjoying my hiss of pain as my abused backside scraped the sheets.

He knelt over me, kissing my throat and my stomach. He nipped at my breasts until I gasped. "Next time," he promised, "I'll touch these rosebuds with my sting." Even the thought of such exquisite punishment made me writhe in trepidation and anticipation, and he chuckled darkly. "Oh, yes, my princess," he growled, "you will dance most divinely for me." And then he spread me open and entered me, trespassing on my body as he had trespassed on the Realm.

I welcomed his violation, as I had welcomed it from the start. Each thrust raked my body across the straw-silk sheets, coarse as a soldier's hands against my raw flesh. I clung to my husband's shoulders and looked up into his predator-dark eyes as I offered myself up for him to devour.

In that moment, the fire transmuted back into pain and then it shattered into a thousand bright sparks of pleasure as pure as the diamonds of the Realm, and my husband's eyes brimmed with wonder and love, and he cried out as he filled me.

Later, curled into the warmth of his embrace, I thought of my sisters, who I am certain were already planning and plotting, determined to find their way back to the Realm and resume their dancing. Perhaps they mourned my loss or praised me for my sacrifice. Little did they know that I had finally found the dance that I had been searching for: a dance of pain and fire, a dance of predator and prey, a dance of soldiers and surrender.

THE SMITH UNDER THE HILL

Kathleen Tudor

Jules tugged at her bodice strings, sighing as the tightly laced fabric released and she took her first really deep breath since lunchtime. Beyond the curtain that divided the front of her booth from the back, she tossed the bodice onto a camp chair and grabbed one of the Tupperware bins they used to store their merchandise. "Can't you help me put this stuff away, Josh? I'm tired." Her twin brother lay on a lounge chair that she suspected he'd stolen from the pool deck of a nearby motel.

"I don't feel well," he said.

She frowned. "Maybe that's because you're drunk."

"I'm not." That was the trouble. He wasn't, though by all rights he should be. Ever since they'd arrived in town for the Everwood Renaissance Festival, he'd been lethargic and lazy, and had been literally eating and drinking his way through every dollar they made. Just today he'd been back to the ale stand probably a dozen times, but she was dead certain that he was as sober as she was. It was weird.

"The customers are gone. You don't even have to get dressed." He rolled over, turning his back to her, and she had to close her eyes and count to ten before she could turn and take the bin out to the front tables.

She was packing up hammered bracelets, muffling each in a fold of cotton cloth, when a gypsy in swirling robes paused to sigh over one of the high-end daggers. "You have darkness in your aura. What troubles you, my child?"

"I'm just worried about my brother." And our business.

Sally blinked. "I'd forgotten he was here. Is he sick or something? I haven't seen him..."

"He's been lying around refusing to do anything since we got here. And I can't work the forge *and* deal with customers."

"Do you mind if I go back and see him?"

Jules waved her through and continued her work. She was going to have to work more hours at the forge, which meant she was going to have to stay up late tonight, too. She could make some earrings fairly quickly, and supplement some of the more intensive items with a larger stock of wire-wrapped jewelry....

She turned to glance at the little forge they'd set up, and was shocked to find Sally standing at it, using a heavy leather glove to pluck a bar of iron out of the coals. "What are you doing?" Jules started toward her, but Sally turned and hurried through the curtain to the camp, carefully holding the fabric away from the hot iron. Jules came through behind her just in time to see Sally touch the heated tip of the iron to Josh's bare arm.

Jules screamed, but Josh didn't. Instead, he jumped up like an angry cat, positively bristling as he leapt away from Sally and...did he *hiss* at her? His arm wasn't blistered or blackened at all, and Jules froze, her breath gone as she struggled to understand.

"He's not Josh," Sally said.

"*What*?" Jules said, and at the same time Josh screeched, "Bitch!"

Then he was gone. Just...gone.

"*What the fuck*?" She was going to be sick.

"It wasn't Josh," Sally repeated, looking sheepishly down at the bar. "I should probably put this back."

Jules stood frozen in place until Sally returned. "You need to explain to me what just happened. Where did my brother go?"

Sally shrugged, still looking sheepish. "Faerie."

It took Jules a minute to process that. "If this is a practical joke, it's the worst one in history. Josh! Where are you? Your little prank is sinking our business, you twit!"

"He's not here, but I might be able to help you. When did this all start?"

"I don't know, when we *got* here!"

"But was there anything more specific? Anything that he ate or drank or somewhere he went that you didn't?"

Jules shook her head, ready to kick Sally out of her camp, when she remembered. "The party..." Sally nodded for her to continue, so, feeling ridiculous, she said, "There was a big party out in the hills the night we got here. We could hear the music from our camp. Josh went to check it out, and he didn't come back until dawn. I wasn't surprised when he slept all day, but he's been like that ever since..."

"That was no normal party; I think there's a faerie hill out there. Your only chance to get him back is to bargain with them. I can help you."

It couldn't be true. It was make-believe. Stories. A prank. But Jules had put that iron in the fire herself—it was hot enough to brand, and Josh hadn't been burned. He hadn't even seemed hurt, just...angry. Josh. Not Josh. Faerie.

"How did you know?"

"I've been there." Sally chewed her lip. "I'm half-blood," she admitted. "They cast me out. But I know their tricks, and I'll help you."

Jules went out into the dark of night, heading toward the hills, and although she was expecting it, she was still surprised to hear the sounds of music and merriment coming from the empty hillsides. She shivered as she moved toward the sound, and nearly screamed when the hillside seemed to crack open above her, creating a cave that nature had never put there.

"Okay, Jules, just relax. Breathe." She climbed to the opening and heard the promise of pleasure drifting out from within. Just before she stepped over the threshold, she remembered what Sally had told her, and plucked the fine silver dagger from her belt.

With her luck, this was just some prank, or some plot to steal her showpiece. She took one last long look at the worked silver, and then knelt and plunged the dagger into the earth at the opening to the cave. "It will hold the entry open for you," Sally had said. Jules sure fucking hoped so.

She turned a corner, and bright light blinded her—light that shouldn't have been there, that *hadn't* been there a moment before. *I'm going crazy*, she decided. It was the only explanation for the sight of a hundred or more beautiful people swirling past in the middle of some chaotic dance, all wearing ball gowns and suits representing a dozen or more eras. *Stark raving. Holy shit.*

And there, working on something that looked like silver with a tiny hammer, at the foot of a dais on the far side of the room, was her brother. He looked haggard, with his beard growing in and dark circles under his eyes, but he stared at the little piece of metal with absolute intensity.

"Josh!"

At her cry, the music stopped and every form on the dance

floor stopped and turned to her in unison, their eyes hungry and predatory. They seemed to lean toward her, and Jules had to fight the urge to flee. Sally's words whispered in her head, and she shook herself. "You took my brother. I—I come to claim him."

The crowd parted to admit the most beautiful man she'd ever seen. His hair was the rich brown of roasted coffee or fertile soil, and his eyes were as green as a leafy canopy. He was tall and slender, but the smooth curves and bulges of muscle showed through.

"And if we don't want to give him up?"

"I'll—um, I'll stay. I'll trade places. Just let him go."

"We'll consider it," the man said. Faerie trickery, Sally had called it. He'd be expecting the hill to close up behind her. He was going to distract her until she was trapped. But he didn't know she'd wedged his front door open, so it was up to *her* to distract *him* until he was asleep and she could get Josh away.

She reached a shaking hand out, and he took it, whirling her into the madness of a dance that began again, out of nowhere. Through it all, Josh hadn't looked up once from the silver he was working. *Oh god,* Jules thought, *my brother is nuts, and I'm dancing with faeries.*

She thought she was about to die of exhaustion when her dance partner, who Jules had learned was the prince of this little court, led her to a pile of pillows on the dais. Mere feet away from her, Josh sweated over some sort of cloak pin, hammering it into intricate detail.

"Come, my newest delight, drink to our bargain!" the faerie man said, holding a wineglass out to her. Jules tore her eyes from her brother and put a hand up in refusal, though she was parched.

"Thank you, but I couldn't," she said. It was tempting,

though, and for more reasons than thirst. He was glorious and beautiful, and she thought she could get lost in his eyes. He noticed her admiring, and took her hand to kiss her palm. Damn, his lips were as soft as flower petals as they brushed across her skin, and her body responded with the heat of a forge fire.

Sally had warned her about eating or drinking anything, but was sex off the table? Jules blushed at the thought, which only made her prince smile wider. But not calculatingly—there was none of the spider in his expression, like there had been when he offered her the wine. Like there was again, when he lifted a tray of some sort of bread that smelled like honey. She shook her head again, and turned away, but he shifted until he was nearly touching her, sending sparks through every point where his skin and hers were close.

"What is your name, sweet mortal girl?"

"Jules," she whispered.

"Ah, how delightful, for you are indeed a rare and precious jewel. I should have a setting forged for you!"

"That sounds like a cage," she said. This place was messing with her head. She was dizzy and so tired, and it was hard to focus…to remember…god, he was beautiful. She lay back on the pillows to look up at him, smiling as he traced a soft hand up her side beneath her shirt.

"Ah, but a cage of gold and silver. Would it be so bad, little jewel, to find yourself prized and displayed?"

It should. It was hard to remember why she should care. But some of her sense came back to her when he cupped the heat between her legs, and his thumb began to ease toward her zipper. "Not in front of everyone!"

"They won't look if I don't want them to."

"Still, not here."

The prince grabbed her and pulled her on top of him, and they rolled over once, tumbling together among the pillows. She felt twice as dizzy, and for a moment her vision seemed to blur. And then they were in a private room, luxuriously decorated and lit only by a crackling fire, and the sounds of merriment were distant.

"And now?" he asked. He'd landed above her, and his body was hot against hers.

In answer, she lifted up and kissed him, embracing his heat the way she embraced the forge—with cautious delight. Then he pushed up from her and moved down her body to pull her clothing away, and she realized that he'd done something to send his own clothes away. His muscles bunched with every movement, and she admired his strong lines in the glow of the fire, moaning when he tossed her shoes and then her pants away and breathed hot puffs of air on her bare, sensitive skin.

He peeled her shirt and bra away next, and his soft, slender fingers plunged into her hot folds at the same moment that his searing mouth sucked her nipple in. She moaned and opened beneath him as his clever fingers found that special place inside her and his sharp teeth grazed over one sensitive nipple and then the other.

"This shall be your setting, my little jewel." He stroked his fingers inside her and she cried out again as pleasure sparked through her faster than it ever had before. *Talk about a magic touch!* Her body moved by itself, her hips rising to demand more, and he chuckled as his thumb found her clit, making her sob as the pleasure mounted.

"Yes," she whispered, knowing he would take it as agreement. She'd probably have said anything to keep him from stopping. "Yes! Please! Yes!" The pleasure crested and burned through her, and she screamed as it tossed her about like a boat on a stormy sea. Her body shook and convulsed with the pleasure he'd wrought, and she thought, for a moment, that she'd lose her mind completely to the intensity of it. Then he bit down hard on the inner curve of one breast, and she cried out in a mix of pleasure and pain, even as it anchored her once again.

He shifted to poise himself above her, but Jules had other ideas. The pleasure was almost too much, and she needed some control or she'd be lost. She hooked one leg behind his and pushed with her surprising strength, and the prince toppled off with her following. She stopped above him, her grin feeling as hungry and feral as the smiles she'd gotten from the dancing host. He grinned back, and she reached between them to feel the hot stiffness of him, thick and ready. She touched him gently, conscious of the calloused roughness of her hands as she stroked and teased and ran her fingers through the dark curls at its base.

"And will *you* mount *me*, little jewel?" he asked, laughter in his tone. She leaned forward to close her mouth over his, sweeping her tongue softly over his lips before she plunged in. And as she thrust into his mouth, she dropped her hips, thrusting him deep within her. He moaned into her kiss, apparently content to let her play, and she rocked her hips against him, letting him fill her and stretch her. It was as if he'd been made just to pleasure her, and she wondered how much was happy happenstance, and how much was the subtle art of faerie glamour making her feel things she'd never expected to feel.

Either way, her toes curled and her entire body began to tingle as she rode him, her nails digging into his chest as he grinned up at her. She gasped and shuddered as the pleasure grew, and pushed away, holding off, letting it grow. This was absolutely going to kill her. She didn't give a damn.

She was close—so close her whole body shook like a leaf—

when the prince grabbed her hips and lifted her up an inch or two with that hidden strength she'd noticed. She cried out in wordless dismay as she hovered on the brink of orgasm, but that dismay was quickly shattered by the splintering force of ecstasy as he thrust into her, hard and fast, pounding up into her again and again as she screamed in the throes of the most pleasure she'd ever felt, or even imagined.

She was aware of him groaning with his own release, but the room seemed to be spinning and there was a roaring in her ears, and even her earlobes pulsed with shocks of pleasure so great that it was almost pain. She couldn't think of anything at all until he released her hips, and she collapsed to the side, boneless and spent and absolutely satiated.

The prince smiled at her. "I hope you're not through, already?"

"Not at all," Jules said, still struggling for breath. "Shall we try something new?" She reached down to her discarded clothes and found the red sash she'd worn like a belt. Still smiling disarmingly at the faerie prince, she twined it around his wrists, but he frowned and pulled away.

"I do not care for red."

Sally had told her that red threads could bind the fae's powers. "Come on, my prince, make your little jewel happy," she purred, pulling his hands together again and twining the sash around his wrists once more. This time he let her, though he clearly longed to pull free. "So sweet," she whispered. She'd intended to truss him up and leave him, now that the noise from the party seemed to have died, but... "You won't regret it."

She nipped his nose, unable to resist spending just a little more time in her handsome prince's bed, and trailed her nails from his bound wrists, now firmly attached to his headboard, all the way to his chest. Her scratches left red marks all down his muscled arms, and he groaned and strained beneath her, and his muscles bulged as he tested the bonds and they held.

"Now I can do anything I want with you," she said, the taste of power growing sweet on her tongue, like honey. She shuddered with the pleasure of it and moved her hands lower, pinching the little beads of his nipples hard enough to make him hiss and growl.

She should leave, she knew, but his body was hard and hot beneath her, powerful, but under her power, and she laughed as she realized that instead of putting her under his spell, he'd fallen under hers. Or maybe they were under each other's. His cock bumped against her slickness as it swelled, and she moaned and leaned down, biting his neck as she rubbed herself against him. Once more. Once more before she had to go.

A slow undulation of her hips brought his cock in line with her wet channel once again, and she sank onto him, reveling in the power of the moment as much as in the sensation. She rode him slowly, letting the pleasure build and churn, and watched his face as he strained beneath her, unable to take control as he so obviously longed to do.

She ground against him, and her body trembled as she played upon the immense pleasure that she was carefully cultivating. "Still think I'm just good to look at?" she asked, rolling her hips.

The prince groaned and a shudder started up near his shoulders and moved down his body. "Never! You are a queen! A goddess!"

Jules laughed and quickened her pace just a little—just enough—until the pleasure overwhelmed her and sent her into convulsions of ecstasy that left her spinning and weak with satiation.

"Release me! Please!"

"What will you give me?" she asked, breathing hard, her fingers already toying with the knots.

"Anything! Anything!"

She laughed as she freed him, and as soon as the red sash dropped away from his skin he grabbed her, moving almost faster than she could follow until he was atop her, pounding hard, his eyes feral with desire. She cried out beneath the assault as he wrung yet more pleasure from her exhausted body, and he followed a moment later, roaring in triumph as he seated himself deep within her and his entire body went taut with his release.

Then he lowered himself beside her and they lay, sweaty and tangled up with each other as their breathing slowed. She waited until his was deep and steady with the rhythms of sleep, and then with a strange sensation of regret she crept out of the bed to hurry into her clothes.

From her pants pocket she plucked a little silver cross on a silver chain, and slipped it over her head, tucking it into her shirt. Then she found the door and snuck out, praying that Josh wouldn't be too hard to find.

The ballroom was at the end of the hall, deserted now except for her brother, who still labored over the beautiful piece of silver. She hurried to his side and pulled a second cross from her pocket, putting it around his neck. He blinked then, and looked up from his silver for the first time, turning bleary eyes on her. "Sis?"

"We have to go. Come on." She tugged at his arm and he stumbled to his feet, letting her pull him along behind her. They were almost to the entrance when the prince himself stepped out of a hidden passage, barring their way.

"You would steal what is mine?" he asked, fury in his eyes. His naked body was powerful and gleaming.

"You promised me anything," she reminded him. His eyes narrowed, and she touched the silver at her throat. "Your magic can't touch me. I'm taking my brother. Keep your oath."

He stepped reluctantly aside, just enough that she had to brush against him as she tugged Josh toward the entrance and their escape.

The dagger was still there, plunged into the soil of the hill, and she pushed Josh out ahead of her and stopped to wrap her hand around the silver hilt. And she paused, hesitating, her heart whispering something she didn't really understand. Then from behind her, the cave carried a true whisper to her ears.

"My queen." The prince's voice was mournful. It called to something dark and glorious within her.

She yanked the dagger from the soil and tossed it out into the night, then she stepped back into the darkness as the hill sealed before her eyes, cutting off one last astonished glance from her brother. And in the new darkness, tender hands caressed her arms, inviting her to turn.

"Your queen," she said. Her hands took his and he pressed his palms together within hers in a gesture that she recognized from the Faire as a sign of fealty.

He went to his knees before her, his eyes glittering in the dark, and his voice was the barest whisper, like magic against her skin. "Yes."

THE SEVEN RAVENS

Ariel Graham

When she was born, the doctors came to Cecily's parents and told them not to expect their child to live. Her mother, still sweating and crying from labor, stared in horror at the managed care providers and tried to make herself understand. Her husband, shop clerk by day, wizard by night, went hard, his muscles tense, his jaw working as he started to chant.

"Don't," Cecily's mother said. "Please. She's just got here. Don't let her come into a world where you're—doing that." *Doing that* was her way around saying "magic" or "casting a spell." Cecily's mother didn't believe in magic. What Cecily's mother believed in was the small bundle of baby the doctors brought and placed in her trembling arms.

Cecily stared at her mother with pacific blue eyes. She'd been born with a hole in her heart, a condition that might heal, a condition that might not heal. Whatever her chances, the managed care providers had options and choices, and all of those options and choices came with price tags.

Cecily's father clenched his fists and tried hard to make money pour from the sky, or the cheap hospital silverware turn into gold, or for Cecily to heal spontaneously, but there are some things magic can't change.

They took her home with them, into the nursery they'd prepared with green baseboard and sky-blue walls, with yellow curtains like the sun and murals of birds flying. Cecily's father's best friend and his family, all of them raven haired and white skinned, lived next door, in an identical home in a cookie cutter subdivision. Cecily's father's best friend and his wife came to visit, bringing with them home-cooked meals, infant mobiles and the promise that someday, somehow, their families would unite. Through friendship. Or marriage.

For a week Cecily's parents lived in the wonder of Cecily, until the night her temperature rose, her cheeks flushing, her fists waving in infant fury.

"Send for a doctor," Cecily's mother said. "I don't want to move her. I don't want to take her out of the house." It was snowing outside, a deep January snow, the kind that erases streets and houses and buildings and leaves only white baffling that deadens voices and hope.

Cecily's father didn't want to leave Cecily's mother. He didn't want to leave his child's side. Terrified that his daughter would die, Cecily's father called his best friend and asked if he and his family would run and get help. If each went a to different source, their number of chances would increase.

"Help is coming," Cecily's father said to Cecily's mother when he went back into the nursery.

But help never came. Cecily's father's best friend's family panicked and lost their way in the snow. In their panic, they searched for hospitals and doctors but found closed restaurants and shuttered churches and abandoned gas stations. It was as if the snowstorm had changed the city into an unfamiliar, haunted place.

They returned without a doctor.

"We'll take a cab," Cecily's mother said, brushing past her husband with the baby swaddled in her arms. "Damn the out-of-program costs. I'm getting help."

Cecily's father agreed. His daughter had a hole in her heart. He had to do whatever he could to bring her fever down.

On the front porch, Cecily's father paused and stared up at the sky. There were birds overhead, wild and free as his daughter might never grow to be. He didn't know what had happened to his best friend's family, or why help never came, but he felt powerless and angry.

His wife turned back just before she reached the cab, the word *No* on her lips. Too late.

Cecily's father cursed his best friend's family, causing his children to take the form of ravens and not know the comfort of human society. In his panic, he misspoke the curse. His best friend's daughter was spared.

He followed his wife into the cab, ducking his head and sheltering his infant daughter from the snow.

Twenty-Four Years Later

On her twenty-fourth birthday, Cecily ran a marathon to prove she could. She celebrated with friends, with her family, and with her father's best friend's wife and daughter; her father's best friend had left the family years ago. Cecily had never known him.

"Where are you going?" her mother asked when Cecily started for the door just short of midnight. Even after twenty-four years, her mother worried.

"Just out to the porch for fresh air." Cecily was tall and blonde, beautiful and athletic. Tonight she was restless. Something had bothered her all day, something about the way her father's best friend's wife had watched her at her birthday dinner.

"Maybe she just thought it was weird I don't have a boyfriend," Cecily muttered to herself. She certainly thought it was odd, and something she'd like to rectify. She was twenty-four and groping in cars and meeting in college boys' filthy dorm rooms had gotten old. She wanted a boyfriend, a relationship and a life.

And she wanted something else. As she leaned against the porch rail, keeping neatly back out of the January snow, she let the desire build. For the last couple of years she'd dreamed of darkness.

Cecily shuddered in the dark. Even the cold couldn't stop her restless thoughts. In the dark, she imagined hands, touching her, hands that could touch any part of her. That could violate. Hands that could shame. Hands that would punish and spank and leave her naked and vulnerable. She imagined being tied, her hands pulled far from her breasts, her legs pulled far from each other. Powerless, she lay while faceless people stalked around her, touching, looking, laughing, filming. They held implements—dildos, vibrators, anal plugs, wooden spoons, hairbrushes, riding crops—and nothing she said could keep them from her. She had no will.

She'd given up her will. She'd consented.

The notion of consenting—to anything, to everything, to pain and pleasure, humiliation and punishment—left her weak. Breathless.

"Cecily?"

"Be right in, Dad."

But she wandered to the edge of the porch and stood a moment longer, staring into the darkness of the winter's night.

From the night around her came a voice. "Cecily."

She started. "Daddy?"

But she knew better.

"Cecily."

"Who are you?" Her heart pounded against her ribs, her breath came short, but she wasn't afraid. She was...curious. Certainly not hopeful. Of course her fantasies were only fantasies.

He stepped out of the pools of darkness that lay between the streetlights. He was tall, her father's age, his face lined with experience. Broad shoulders and somehow cunning hands. He moved those hands, and stardust fell from his fingers.

Cecily watched and saw a story begin to form.

"Once, you would not have been alone on this night. Our families were joined in friendship and tonight you would have been joined by boyfriend, friend, mentor, confidant, playmate, tormentor and lover."

She should be afraid, she thought. But standing in the dark, talking to a man she thought might be her father's long-lost best friend, she was only curious.

"I don't understand. I thought you only had a daughter?" Her father's best friend's daughter still lived next door with her father's best friend's ex-wife. She wasn't very nice, and Cecily had little to do with her.

"Now," he said. "Now I only have a daughter. But once I had more children." His voice held sorrow, and something else—a thrill of anger.

Cecily stepped forward instead of back, and put one hand on his arm. "Tell me," she said, and that is how Cecily learned that her father had cursed his best friend's family, turning young male restlessness into black winged ravens. Seven ravens, and seven keys which her father's best friend offered to Cecily on the flat of his hand. Seven keys that could break the curse.

One key opened a mountain of glass.

One key created a map.

One key led to heaven.

One key led to hell.

One key unlocked pleasure.

One key unlocked pain.

One key spoke the spell that would transform ravens back into humans, seven who might be Cecily's boyfriend, friend, mentor, confidant, playmate, tormentor and lover.

Each key came with a price.

She took the keys without question. She left the porch without thought. She went into the city in search of ravens.

The city was deserted. Another January snowstorm had caused a power failure and at midnight the streets were empty and impassable. Snow transformed the asphalt and concrete, the cars and buildings soft-edged and unreal. The snow muffled sound. No planes flew that night. No cars ran. No subways chugged. The streets were empty. Cecily's boots left tracks in the otherwise virgin snow.

She walked down the street, looking up at the snow that fell from the dull gray post-midnight sky. She carried the seven keys in her hands, wondering at the size and shape of them and what she was to do. Find a mountain made of glass, find a map, unlock heaven, unlock hell, learn pleasure and pain. Speak the spell that would release the ravens.

Snowflakes fell on her eyelashes and cheeks. She looked up toward the swirling sky and saw the mountain made of glass. The tallest building in the city, easily fifty stories tall, it glowed despite the power failure, all steel and glass, a seat of financial power.

She didn't question how she knew. She didn't know that she was right. She just walked, heading for the building, the shiniest of the keys outstretched in her hand. Above her, seven ravens whirled in flight, following her down through the double glass doors into the marble lobby and into the shining steel elevator. She took the car up to the penthouse, stepped out into silence and glass and the city, dead and white below her. The room was full of white furniture and black birds.

"I'm here," Cecily said into the silence and from the darkness came a dark-haired man, hair black as coal, eyes dark as night. Six crows surrounded him, fluttering their midnight feathers, heads cocked to watch her with their oil-drop eyes.

He held his hand out to her with a low bow. "I am the son of your father's best friend. I would have been your boyfriend."

Cecily regarded him. "Do I know you?" She took his hand, let him draw her closer.

"You should."

His lips on hers were warm and soft. He smelled like feathers, warm and spicy. His hands went to her hair, cupped her face, slid down her back, then moved to her ass and pulled her tight against him. She felt his cock, hard against her, straining against the black slacks he wore, and her heart pounded faster.

Her clothes melted away as they might in a dream. The empty office was cold, and she shivered against him as he removed his clothes, letting them fall behind him. He pulled her to one of the white couches, guided her down beneath him. He caressed her breasts, letting his fingers trail out to her nipples, tweaking and pinching, laughing as she pulled away. He bit her neck and she breathed into him, aching for his touch, aching for something else.

His hands slipped down the slope of her hip bones, angled inward. One finger sank farther, touched her clit, slid between her lips. His breathing was rough and fast.

Cecily pressed against him, felt his cock against her naked belly, felt his fingers sinking into her cunt, probing, sliding, fucking her until her head fell back and her breathing all but stopped.

He pushed himself up on rigid arms, stared into her face, and he was familiar and a stranger, all at once.

"Spread your legs."

She blushed and moved them apart. He angled himself and sank deep inside her, his back arching as he pumped into her, hard, with very little rhythm, just need, as if he had missed her for so very many years.

Heat built in Cecily, warming her core, spreading from cunt and clit, spiraling up until she thought she'd burst with tension, with anticipation, and then she came for the first time with someone else there. Her head tipped back against the arm of the couch, and she screamed as waves of pleasure battered her.

"I would have been your boyfriend," he whispered in her ear and then he was gone, the ravens were gone, the room was empty and Cecily stood alone in the penthouse of the mountain of glass.

She pocketed the key and took the elevator back down to the marble lobby.

On the street again, she went looking for the map that would lead her to the son of her father's best friend, the one who would have been her friend.

Outside the glass and steel skyscraper she found the city map, a laminated and under-Plexiglas thing, battered despite protection, and seeming to indicate a city Cecily doubted resembled the one she was in.

The skeleton key in her hand fit the map stand, and when she opened it another map appeared, bright and primal and promising heaven.

He came up behind her, dark as his brother had been, and took her elbow.

"You shouldn't be out on the street at night," he said, guiding her toward a garden set between two of the steep buildings. There was little snow there, and the summerhouse was wound with morning glory vines. Six ravens followed them, swooping down to land noisily on the summerhouse roof, feathers twitching, beady eyes watching. Cecily felt warmer out of the never-ending snow.

"Do I know you?" He looked so like the man she had met before, the boyfriend, but of course they had to be brothers.

"I would have been your friend." His dark eyes were warm. He watched her, ready to laugh or cry at her desire.

"What's the price for knowing you now?"

"A kiss," he said, a Peter Pan request, and the ravens around them laughed rustily.

Cecily leaned up on her toes and kissed him on the cheek. The next instant he was gone.

She entered the summerhouse, her boots leaving snow on the steps to melt as spring triumphed over the January night. Inside, a black-haired, dark-eyed man stood watching her. His mouth quirked in a smile. He held one hand out to her, and Cecily took it, letting him lead her to a chaise swathed with silks. From somewhere she heard strains of music. She was warm and happy and unafraid.

One key unlocked heaven.

"Do I know you?" she asked. He looked like the boyfriend, and the friend. How many sons had her father's best friend had? No one had spoken of it in her house. No one had spoken of it in her father's best friend's ex-house.

"I would have been your mentor." He urged her down onto the chaise, and when she struggled to stand again, he pressed her shoulders down, keeping her there.

"You have got to learn your place. You have got to learn."

Her cheeks burned as the stranger undressed himself, revealing alabaster skin, a lean chest, long arms, hard abs and finally a jutting cock, long and thick and hard for her. When she tried to turn her head away, tried to stand, he caught her face between his palms. Standing above her, he pressed his cock against her lips, pushing, guiding, forcing her mouth open.

Cecily's gaze rose to meet his. She opened her mouth and let him slide his length inside her. He tasted salty and musty, like deep-red wine, heated, with spices. He was already slick with precome, and when he pressed forward the head of his cock bumped the back of her throat.

"Open your throat. Let me in. Let me fuck you." He held the back of her head and rocked his hips into her. Cecily groaned, then let herself relax, opening to him, wrapping her tongue around his cock, sucking, hollowing her cheeks, letting him fill her as the fire between her legs grew again, not satiated. She wanted him; she wanted his hands, his cock, his tongue.

She wanted everything she'd had tonight, the sex, the friendship, the control.

The ravens watched from corners of the room, shifting noisily.

Cecily moved forward and back, sucking hard, feeling the man above her tense as he started to come. He pulled back suddenly, pulling himself free of her mouth. His come splattered across her face, into her hair.

"You're learning," he said, when she didn't reach up to wipe her mouth. "Go clean up." He pointed to a door in the back of the summerhouse. It hadn't been there when they'd entered. He followed her, at least as far as the door, which was locked. She fumbled with the seven keys in her hand, pulling one out that was a curious dull red, scorched by fire, perhaps.

One key leads to heaven. One would lead to hell.

The red key opened the door in the back of the summerhouse. The seven ravens swept through it with her, ruffling her hair, disturbing the air in the hot room. The door slammed shut behind her and Cecily knew without checking the door would be locked.

He stood in front of her, tall, strong, muscled, dark. He didn't smile, but held out his hand. The room around him was a stage set for play, the kind of thing she only let herself dream of in her most private moments.

Cecily's cheeks heated with shame. She wanted what was there.

One key would lead to hell.

"Do I know you?" she asked the muscular man. He had rolled up his sleeves over corded forearms and stood waiting for her. He looked so familiar, like a dream she might have had, or like the boyfriend, friend and mentor she had met.

"I would have been your confidant. Tell me your deepest fears. Your secrets." He whispered: "Your wants."

Her eyes swept the room. She wanted it all, the dungeon look, the exhibition, the pain, the punishment, the release. She wanted the crops and belts and canes and cats. She wanted him.

"I'm afraid."

"That's a good start."

He didn't offer her his hand again. Instead, he took hers roughly, yanked her to him, pulled her jeans down in a practiced motion and felt between her legs. "You're soaking wet. Smell yourself. Lick my fingers clean."

She tasted of onions, she thought, distracted, and came back to herself when he ordered her to strip. Around her the six ravens muttered and paced.

Her jeans, her panties, her T-shirt, her bra. Defenseless, she faced him, afraid, but wanting.

"Tell me what you fear the most."

She wouldn't, she thought, but her eyes betrayed her, darting fast across the room to fasten on the canes that hung from a peg.

In one fast motion he toppled her across a desk and Cecily thought now it looked like a schoolroom they were in; she wouldn't have been surprised to have a class sitting there watching, to find herself in tartan plaid, but it was just Cecily, naked, vulnerable, watched by the ravens.

"Don't move."

She heard him cross the room. Her breath caught. She held it. This was what she'd waited for.

This was what she'd feared.

It took forever for him to cross the small space, to bring back one of the thin, whippy canes and one of the thick, formidable ones.

She wanted him to make her count. In her darkest moments, she thought the humiliation of keeping her own count would be—sublime? Hellish? Hers.

He was to have been her confidant. Of course he knew.

"Count," he ordered, and then he started. The thick cane cracked down across her ass, hitting the sweet spot. Cecily shouted in surprise and pain, bucked up and felt him shove her back down hard. The sting blossomed and an instant later became searing, red-hot pain.

"Count!" he shouted.

"One!"

"Sir."

"One, Sir!"

The thick cane again, leaving a trail of red; she could feel welts starting and welts over welts. She cried, she kicked; six times the cane descended and then he stopped.

She felt him walk close behind her. His hands came down, mauling her ass, pinching handfuls of reddened, angry flesh. One hand reached down between her legs.

"You're even wetter."

She moaned.

"Six more." And the cane snapped across her skin, leaving marks, leaving trails. She hurt. She screamed. She struggled even as the ravens laughed. Under it all, the need crested, the pleasure built, the pain exploded until Cecily exploded, clit throbbing, cunt pulsing, mouth open as she panted through the orgasm.

He hit her one more time as it faded. She grunted, let her head drop to the desk.

The snow woke her instants later. Snow blowing into the room, chasing away the warmth of heaven, the heat of hell. She wasn't surprised to find herself dressed again. She ached, warmth spreading from her ass to her cunt and clit. She wanted more.

The seven ravens watched her. Another key would lead her to pleasure. Out, then, from the hellish room. There was only one door, and it wasn't the one she'd come in through. She crossed to it, finding a slim silver key that fit the lock. The ravens brushed through ahead of her. Cecily followed and stood in a huge room full of people milling about. Instantly she glanced down at herself, but her clothes were still there, jeans and a T-shirt, boots and keys. She searched then, until she found him.

He was grinning, mischievous and cute, with sharper features than the others, but just as dark of hair, pale of skin, just as tall and strong and just as much in control of Cecily.

She wanted to say she'd already figured it out this time but her mouth shaped the words. "Do I know you?"

"I would have been your playmate."

She thought initially that would have meant something else. Now she just took his hand and allowed him to lead her up onto a stage at the end of the room. Now the guests in the room turned and looked at the ravens fluttering above them, then up to the stage where Cecily's playmate removed her clothes.

"Show them," he said.

She stared at him, her hands protectively over breasts, legs twisting together.

He laughed at her. "Oh, no. No." He took her hands away from herself and walked her into the lights at the edge of the stage. Standing behind her he offered up her breasts to the crowd, pushed her hips forward and separated her lips, turned her and bent her and spread her legs and all the while the guests assembled sipped their drinks and petted each other and laughed and commented and asked if they could touch.

"No," her playmate said. "She's all mine."

His touch tickled. He stroked and nipped, he kissed and licked, he squeezed her aching ass and slid a finger into her asshole and wouldn't let her go when she tried to squirm away. He tickled her and stoked her and bit her and told her she was beautiful and the fire inside her climbed again. Cecily fed off the crowd, ashamed and frightened and excited and abandoned. She reached down for his cock, hard inside his black slacks, rubbed him hard and laughed when he pushed her away, went right back to it until he turned her, tucked her butt into his crotch, bent her and reached his arms around to play with her clit.

"Come. Come for the nice people. Let them see your face when I make you come."

Cecily screamed, head dropping, her entire body convulsing. She heard the guests laugh, some of them applaud; she heard groans and sighs as the assembled personages lost their clothes and their minds and pleasure rippled through the room.

"I want to stay here," Cecily said, eyeing the ravens. Five of them circled.

"I won't let you," her tormentor said, tearing her from the arms of her playmate. He forced her fingers around the spiky iron key and dragged her to the door across the stage, the one that lead to pain.

A plain, utilitarian room, where six ravens circled, cawing. Cecily shrank back. In the center of the room stood the bed, four poster, empty of covers, only rough rope ties on the posts. He dragged her to it, threw her down faceup, grabbed her arms and legs and tied her. Struggling did no good. He was stronger. He was impossibly faster.

"Please!" Cecily begged her tormentor as the fire inside her grew again. This had been one of the dark dreams. This had been the hidden shameful fantasy. This had been the want, the need, the desire. The question. Could she?

And now, this was the reality.

He held a cane: slim, black, long. Held it for her to see, laughed as she watched when he brought it down slowly and dipped it into her cunt. Her juices coated it. Her clit throbbed, aching for touch. Her cunt pulsed at the tip of the cane.

He laughed, and lifted the cane, and brought it down across her nipples.

Cecily screamed in pain as sting became burn.

And burn became pleasure.

And pleasure became pain again. He struck her thighs, her breasts, her mons. He laughed as she cried, and laughed as she squirmed, and laughed when he pushed the cane between her legs, and let her ride it until she screamed again, this time coming.

He left her there, tied spread-eagled, sweating and shaking, crying a little, until the pain and pleasure both ebbed and then he unknotted the ropes and let her stand.

She wasn't dressed this time. She didn't care. There was only one key left, a black one shaped like a raven's wing. She carried it with her across the room, stumbling a little, making little cries of want and fear. She stopped at the black barred door of heavy wooden timbers, iron marking the shape of a raven across it.

One key led to the spell that would transform raven to human, and now she might find boyfriend, friend, mentor, confidant, playmate, tormentor and lover.

Seven ravens flew in over her head. The room looked like her parents' living room in the house she had grown up in, the house next door to her father's best friend's house where he'd lived with his wife and daughter. But once, he'd said, he'd had more children. Seven sons? Or only one?

The key would fit the front door that led to the porch where her father had stood when he cursed his best friend's children. When she turned it, the door opened to snow and darkness. Here she would find the spell.

She didn't know what the spell was. Didn't know what she was supposed to find.

But her father had cursed them.

Cecily blessed them.

"Blessed be."

There was a ruffle of feather behind her at the entrance to the house. Cecily turned slowly to see the seven dark haired men standing in the doorway. One would be her lover.

The seventh stepped forward and held out his hand.

Cecily reached for him and one after another the seven fell into a line, each so hard on the heels of the one before him they seemed to be tumbling together like dominos, not knocking into each other but falling inside each other, these raven-haired men who looked so alike.

Cecily's father's best friend had said he had more children, not how many more. She held her breath, childish and wanting the boyfriend, friend, mentor, confidant, playmate, tormentor and lover.

He stood before her, one man, dark hair, pale skin. He held his hand out to her and there was no door to go through, no key to unlock secrets, turn curses. They were together, and the curse was breaking.

There was one man, one father's best friend's son.

"Are you the one I've been waiting for?" she asked. The question sounded naïve to her own ears, but what could she do other than ask?

The raven-haired man pulled her close, his embrace a combination of need and want, request and demand. He held her as if she were precious and with a fierce roughness that sent her heart racing.

"I've been waiting for you," he said.

Cecily frowned. "There were seven," Cecily said, uncertain if she felt afraid or greedy or hopeful.

"Friend, boyfriend, mentor, confidant, playmate, tormentor, lover. What use is a husband who is not all those things?"

Cecily tilted her head and studied him. The night passing behind them seemed a dream, but she remembered it clearly.

"Seven ravens," she said. "Seven sons, seven keys."

"Seven aspects," he corrected.

They were alone in the house, all seven rooms to themselves.

"Let me show you," her friend said. He took her hand and led her to the bedroom, and there his kiss trapped her mouth under his, hot and intimate as the boyfriend held her, stroking her hair, whispering to her.

Cecily let her head fall back, let him hold her as he tugged at her clothes, laughing when he tangled her in her T-shirt and bra. Her boyfriend kissed her neck and bit her ears and whispered what he wanted to do to her.

Cecily felt molten, wet and wild; her hands stroked him through his jeans. His cock was hard and familiar. She wanted him, now, and she willingly complied when her mentor told her what he wanted.

"Down on your knees, don't use your hands." He freed himself from the button-fly jeans, his cock rigid, straining toward her. She opened her lips, let him press between them. He was salty and silky in her mouth, huge and forceful and Cecily gave herself over to instruction, to his hands that pressed her head against him, to his words, low and throaty, telling her to take it deep. She hollowed her cheeks, sucked and let her tongue play, and when he came, filling her mouth, she swallowed and gasped and let her confidant pull her to her feet.

"That's what you like, isn't it?" he asked. "Being controlled? Nothing left up to you? Nothing you could do about it? Tell me."

She leaned close to him, tumbling them both down to the huge arctic bed, all white jersey sheets and white microfiber blankets, white as the snow that filled the world on her birthday.

"I want it," she said. "I want all of it. I want everything. I want to do everything. I want to be told."

"Everything?" her playmate asked, and pulled her on top of him, hands exploring, teasing feathery fingertip touches along the insides of her hip bones and along her lips, down into her wet folds. He pulled her up to straddle him, the two of them sideways on the enormous white bed, and slid deep inside her.

Cecily gasped, her eyes closing.

"Do you like this?" her playmate asked, fingertips brushing down the slope of her breasts.

She nodded, inarticulate.

"Do you like this?" her tormentor asked, his fingers tightening, tweaking, pulling, stretching her nipples until she made another sound, of pain and want.

"Tell me." He bit her breast. "Tell me." An open-handed slap across her ass as she rode him.

"Tell me." As the two of them came together, Cecily and her lover, in the arctic bed as the snow fell outside the house, the curse lifted.

BLACK OF KNIGHT

Victoria Blisse

I wasn't supposed to believe in magic. I was a lady and such fanciful thought wasn't encouraged; in fact thinking wasn't held to be healthy for a princess at all. I thought a lot. I hadn't always been a princess. The story is a long and drawn out tale with the usual dragon vanquished by a shining knight in too much armor, so here is the shortened version.

Truth be told, the dragon hadn't been particularly evil; he just got lonely. As long as I snuggled up with him at bedtime, and scratched any itches he might have, I was left to my own devices most of the time. I roamed the forest without fear because everyone knew I was the dragon's daughter and no creature would harm me because they feared the consequences.

I talked to whomever I liked, when I liked: animals, fairies, pixies and even the odd troll. Then there was the handsome man who had wandered too deep into the trees that day. He had striking blue eyes under darker hair than mine, and his lip quirked to one side when he smiled. That had been a good day; it had been my eighteenth birthday.

It wasn't long after that the shiny knight came. It was difficult to explain to him that I might have been a damsel, but the only distress I was in was at his manhandling of me. I told him I loved the dragon and that he wasn't a cruel master but my father. I don't think the words pierced the metal of his helmet.

I yelled to the dragon in his own tongue to escape. I told him that the knight would fight, and such a scrawny thing was destined to get lucky and find the dragon's one weak spot, because that is how those things work. The dragon, as wise as his hundreds of years, lumbered up, making the ground tremble. He then took to the sky for the first time in god alone knew how long and flew away, crying burning hot tears all the way. I wept too, but my tears didn't boil, more's the pity.

So I was taken back to the castle by this very pleased and pompous man with thin lips and so much pride it leaked like grease through his pores. I was presented to the king and queen, then thoroughly inspected. I caused quite the stir as I was clothed in the gifts of nature, nothing more. The fairies had sewn me a pretty and practical dress from a certain blossom that was strong and almost completely stain proof. It was also a tad transparent, but as I'd wandered around for years in the nude I thought nothing of that. I'd only worn it that day because I'd been searching out blackberries for a pie and it protected me from the prickle of thorn and the purple stain of juice.

I was poked at by strange and bony fingers and the little blemish above my ankle—which I had always thought looked like a tiny dragon's paw—was declared to be the mark of the crown and I was welcomed back as Princess Eloise, the long-lost daughter of the king and queen.

I tried to escape a few times back in the early days, but to no avail. I wept, I hardly slept and I barely ate either. The food was strange and not charred enough and I missed my best friend in all the world, my father. I would have refused to eat altogether if they hadn't threatened to force-feed me. I just wanted to die. Melodramatic, I know, but when you've had the whole realm of nature as your playground and all the freedom in the world you don't want anything else. I felt trapped; I was a miserable prisoner.

I didn't want to wear the princess dress; I didn't want a stupid little crown. I didn't want to learn to dance, to use a knife and fork and to curtsy. I didn't want to learn to sew. I would have given up on life completely if it hadn't been for one little visitor.

"Pssst…" The noise was like a bee by my ear in the dead of night. I woke up with a groan.

"Pssst, Dragon Daughter, it is I, fae of the Magnolia."

"Maggie," I whispered, "is it really you?"

"Yes, mistress, but I can't stay long. This place holds little magic and it hurts me to be here."

"Tell me your message." I held out my finger and Maggie sat upon it, panting. She let off a slight glow that was sickly green. In the forest she shone brighter than my father's favorite diamonds.

"The dragon sends you his love. He tells you not to worry, he has found a new cave and is settling well. He misses you but wants you to not miss him too much. He says you are a human and should learn to live with humans. It is your place in the world and he should never have stolen you all those years ago, but you were the prettiest jewel he had ever seen and he couldn't help himself."

I choked back a sob and turned my head as tears dripped down my face. Salt water on the fairy's wings would disable her, and she would need all her strength to fly home.

"He says he loves you and he wants you to become the best princess you can be. He'll never forget you."

"Thank you, Maggie," I snuffled. "Tell him I love him and miss him but I will try to do as he commands. I will remain his loving daughter, always."

Maggie squeezed my thumb weakly in reply.

"Take strength, Dragon Daughter, he will always be with you; the power of his love is in your soul."

And she flew away.

So I tried to become a princess. I conquered many embroidery stitches, but found French knots a little tricky, and I learned to curtsy like any of the ladies in waiting. I ate my meals with a knife, fork and spoon and even knew in which order to use them. I allowed the maids to tame my hair into curls and twirls but I would not let them cut my brunette locks. My hair was too useful; it kept me warm at night and when I curled up in its depths I imagined I was back home with the dragon, my father.

Of course, the king was my fairy-tale father; well, he might as well have been a tale for all I saw of him and my brother. They were forever off hunting or being diplomatic, whatever that meant. I didn't see much of my birth mother either. She didn't seem to like me much.

"But Eloise, you must pick a suitor and soon. You are old to still be courting, and you do not want to be left a spinster."

"But your majesty..." I never called her mother, it didn't seem right. "None of the men have heated my loins; they leave me completely dispassionate."

The queen blushed scarlet, which clashed with the light seashell pink of her gown. She wafted her hand in front of her face and pulled her lips together into a fierce pucker. I'd said something wrong again.

"We do not talk about loins, dear. That is impolite and totally unimportant."

"No. I am choosing a mate, a male to plant his seed within me from which a child flower will grow. If a man is to bury his—"

"Say no more, Eloise. We do not discuss such base things." The queen shuddered, her slight frame convulsed with revulsion.

"The prince thinks about his loins all the time. He tups any wench he likes. You are not pressuring him into marriage, and he is not much younger than I."

"No, but he is a man and men have needs. He will settle down when he is ready."

"I have needs too, your majesty. Just because I do not have a prick—"

"Eloise, go to your room. You will be at the maiden's ball tonight and you will pick a suitor. That is the end of the matter."

All the conversations I ever had with the queen ended with her shouting. Many of them started that way too. I went to the stupid ball that night, but I was determined not to pick a suitor.

I defied the maid, the constraints of society and my queen by wearing my hair loose around me. I allowed myself to be cinched into a turquoise-green gown, though. Some things are not worth arguing over. It seemed strange to me that my fairy dress, which covered everything but hinted at my body beneath, was regarded as obscene. The dress I wore that night revealed the majority of my tit flesh—though I had been taught to call it a décolletage—leaving much less to the imagination.

I'd been heaved into a corset and squeezed within an inch of my life. Society had a strange obsession with tiny waists. The dragon told me to be proud of my thickness: it meant I would not snap easily under attack. My waist and thick thighs caused a lot of kerfuffle within the walls of the castle; I was simply too well built to be a princess. And when I asked to wear breeches like the gents, as they seemed such a practical item of clothing, the queen and her lady in waiting both fainted. Someone had clearly tightened their corsets far too much.

The ball was as boring and insipid as all the others I'd been forced to attend. There was music, which was pleasant. It was an echo of the sound of the fairy folk band, but not even half as good. If I had been left to enjoy the food and the music it would have been palatable, but I was made to dance with the simpering men and prevented from eating at all.

I contemplated feigning sickness; it would not be difficult to fall backward into the trestle tables filled with food and cause a stir. The queen would send me to my room to be rid of the embarrassment, and then at least I could be alone. I heard a murmur of swishing skirts and then the shocked inhalation of air and I wondered who could be causing such I stir. I looked to the doorway as the low murmurs of unease turned to screams of terror, and watched people scurry to right and left in a rush to get out of the way of the rearing black charger that filled the huge doorway.

It was a magnificent stallion and when it settled, I could see that the man on its back was clad in armor as dark as his mount, his face covered except for a slight slit for him to see through and a grate over his mouth so he could be heard.

"Give me the dragon's daughter," he roared and my heart leapt. At last, some excitement.

I moved to step forward but was surrounded by a group of knights in dancing tights before I could put my lifted foot back on the floor.

"I'll protect you, lady," one said, and the rest repeated the words as if they were magic talismans that would indeed provide some protection.

I sighed and waited. The man on the charger saw the knot of men around me and urged his mount forward. He was indeed a talented horseman because he easily kept the sinewy strength of the magnificent beast well under his control. The ballroom echoed with space, as the partygoers pressed themselves against the walls. I glanced toward the dais and of course, the queen was on her throne, fainted dead away, surrounded by actual guards with actual swords.

"I would know your beauty anywhere, milady." The smooth grit of the knight's voice wrapped me in bonds of finest silk. A shiver ran down my spine, but it was not completely an unpleasant sensation. I nodded graciously to the mounted man as he pulled his stallion to a stop mere hand spans away from my cowering company of dancing knights.

"You eclipse all others, Dragon Daughter."

"Thank you, milord. But you have me at a disadvantage. You know me yet I do not know how to address you."

"I am the Black Knight and I am here to rescue you."

A gasp echoed around the room as every lady still standing lifted her hand to cover the escaping noise of fear.

"I don't think you are, you scourge!" The knight before me, Percy I think he was called, gallantly stood his ground.

"Oh, I am, dear sir, I am." The Black Knight laughed and pulled on his stallion's reins; the animal reared up and the knights that surrounded me ducked and dived to avoid flailing hooves. I stood perfectly still, unafraid and fascinated by what might happen next. As swiftly as the kingfisher grabs its prey the Black Knight turned his steed, reached down and hooked an arm around my waist. He lifted me up with little effort and placed me sidesaddle on the seat before him.

"Cheerio," he yelled with joy in his voice and we sped off out of the castle and into the night. I held on to his arm as we charged along and tried to get ahold of my emotions. I was certainly scared. The man was strong, charismatic and somewhat menacing. He had kidnapped a princess. But he had said he was rescuing me, and he mentioned my real name, so maybe he wasn't all bad.

I did not know that for sure, though. I could not see him; the night was clouded and when I looked between the gap in his visor all I saw was darkness. He did not speak, but I understood why. His steed was strong, but it carried two bodies through a maze of uneven ground and deep into the forest. He needed his concentration.

I was glad when we came to a stop, as I was chilled to the bone. My hair had offered some little warmth but my dancing gown had not.

"Step inside here, Dragon Daughter, we will rest."

He led me into a cave where I found a stone and sat. My knees wobbled beneath me. He left to see to the horse, like any good master would, and when he returned he took off his helmet and breastplate and set to work lighting a fire. His hair was jet black, darker than the night, and his eyes shone like the sapphires I cherished most in my father's collection.

He said nothing more and all my words seemed lost inside me. I watched as he skilfully lay the wood for a fire, which I noted had been stored at the back of the cave. This man had not kidnapped me on a whim. His body had muscle and warmth, his shoulders were wide, his girth was great. He was made of hard muscle and my loins, that had lain dormant so long, came alive.

The dragon always said I liked to dance with danger. He taught me caution, though, and how not to get caught up in the moment. I took in a deep breath to control myself. What could

I do if this man decided he wanted me? I would be powerless to resist. I shuddered with fear though my treacherous body heated, my nipples hardened and my deep, dark places boiled as I imagined him taking me.

"I'm afraid I cannot offer you eiderdown, but I have these to sleep upon."

The Black Knight pulled some rolled-up skins from the back of the cave. He rolled one out on the floor. "Join me and we'll sleep."

"Thank you," I nodded, "but I must get this blasted corset off first or my back will break. Could you aid me?"

"Certainly," he replied.

He walked behind me and with more brute force than skill, opened the back of my dress. It was probably ruined, but I didn't care.

"What is this torturous contraption?" he muttered as he pulled cords and swore under his breath.

"It is to capture fair maidens, to cut off blood flow to the brain and keep them easy to control."

"I note it did not work with you, milady."

"No," I said, smiling wistfully, "my father encouraged my thinking, and this garment could not undo the swelling of my intellect."

At last the blasted boning fell free and I sighed deeply, my ribs singing with the joy of release.

"You are marked," he said, tracing the red bites of the tightened coils with his thick, warm fingers. "It is barbaric." He continued to trace the lines and I stood stock still, my only movement the heaving of my chest.

"I rather enjoyed the constriction," I replied with a smile, "but I am glad to be free of it."

"You liked being restricted?" His voice was husky with desire.

"I did," I whispered.

He continued to inspect my flesh and when his fingers reached my hips, he tore lower, so that the silken material fell free. I was left exposed, as I never wore undergarments, much to my maid's despair. I was naked but I was not vulnerable. In my skin I was myself once more, Dragon Daughter not Princess Eloise.

The Black Knight moved around my body, his fingers never leaving my flesh. He stopped before me and looked directly into my eyes.

"I may be the scourge of the kingdom," he said, "but I will not take a maiden without her consent, as much as my body roars at me to ravish you right now."

"You want me?" I asked. The words caught in my desire and came out hoarse.

"I do," he replied, hands gripped around my waist, his chest inches from my agitated bosom.

"Then take me." His lips were on mine before my sentence was done. The force of his desire buckled my knees, but he held me close to him. I felt the evidence of his need pressing against my stomach, and I grabbed on to his shoulders through the light material of his shirt and let him ravage me.

"I want to try something, Dragon's Daughter. Do you trust me?"

It was a strange question to ask the woman he had kidnapped, but I eagerly asserted that I did.

"Good."

He picked up my ruined dress and ripped away a strip of silk. He moved to me and wrapped the length around my wrists, tying it with a knot so that I could not separate them. I felt my skin heat and my desire mount at being at his mercy.

He tumbled me carefully to the floor, just upon the skin he'd laid out. He removed his shirt and breeches in a hurry and lay once more beside me before my skin could cool from his amorous attack. I blended into him as far as I could, my hands trapped in bonds and held in place between our bodies. I kissed him back with great ferocity and growled while his lips raked down my throat and his teeth bit into the flesh at the dip beneath my chin.

Not a spot of my body did he leave undiscovered. His fingers, his lips and his tongue investigated every nook, every cranny. I felt his body pressed so tight to mine that I knew it would leave an imprint upon my skin forever. I was alive with feeling, dizzy with sensual delight. He ducked between my thighs and drank from my still pool of lust. I did not know what to do with my hands, but they rose unbidden above my head in a symbol of my submission. He lapped so eagerly but with a gentleness that coaxed ecstasy from my deepest being. My soul sang and my body writhed like gold and silver coins pouring through cupped fingers. It was only then, when I had broken apart into a million pieces, that the Black Knight took his own pleasure.

He rose to his knees and split me around him. I looked into his sparkling eyes as he pressed his manhood against my softness. He pressed in, took my maidenhead and stilled as I adapted to his great length within me. I was invaded, I was breached and I squeezed my muscles around him to feel his full length, hot and unrelenting, within the sanctity of my very being. It was glorious.

He moved with slow, precise strokes at first, then bent over me, hands either side of my shoulders, to flex himself and give him balance to rock harder against my pelvis. I wished I could wrap my hands around him, but he seemed greatly aroused by the view of my bound hands lying uselessly above my head. Our gazes met; I drank him in and slipped my bound hands behind his neck and pulled him to me, kissing his scorching lips and watching the desire blossom and bloom in his eyes.

His pinnacle was a pleasure to witness. He tightened up and roared, his mouth wide, his eyes closed, his hair flying around like a dark mane. He held himself so deep within me as ecstasy poured through him that I knew he'd never fully pull away from me again. He crumbled and the pieces of his soul mixed with the broken bits of mine and they blended to make a new whole, a precious joining of Black Knight and Dragon Daughter.

The Black Knight moved to lie beside me. He untwined the binds from my wrists and kissed the points over my pulse, easing the stiffness there. We lay together, and he pulled another skin over us to preserve our lustful heat.

"You never told me you were a knight when we met in the woods."

"No," he replied, "I was struck dumb by your beauty."

"How did you know I was at the castle?" I asked, burrowing into the warmth and safety of his embrace.

"I went to find you and you were not there. I knew you were Dragon Daughter, you told me, so I went to his lair and it was empty. I am not too proud to say I cried in rage at the sky, ripped apart with grief."

I gently caressed his chest, stroking over the wiry curls that protected his heart.

"A fairy came to me in my distress and told me where to find your father. He told me the whole tale, after I convinced him not to eat me."

I laughed and shook my head. That was my father all over.

"So I came to rescue you on the night of the maiden's ball, and now you are a maiden no more."

"I may no longer be pure but I am yours forever, if you want me." I replied with loving fervor.

"Aye, I do," he replied, kissing my brow, "but I must return you to your father first, for his blessing."

"Indeed." I smiled again. I had smiled more times in the arms of the scourge of the kingdom than I had in the entire time I'd been Princess Eloise. "I cannot wait to see him, I have missed him so much."

The Black Knight squeezed me, and our joint soul resounded with my pain. He understood me completely; he did not need to tell me so. We lay entwined together by the warmth of the crackling fire, and I was beginning to drift toward sleep when something disturbed me.

"Soul of my soul," I whispered, and the Black Knight stirred beside me.

"What is it, desire of my heart?"

"How shall I introduce you to my father? I do not know your name."

"I do not have one," he said, shrugging. "I have always been the Black Knight."

"And I am Dragon's Daughter." I nodded. "Black Knight, I will introduce you to my father by that name. I will tell him you are the savior and the keeper of my soul."

"What better introduction could there be?" He smiled and we lay back, content and sleepy. Magic and love entwined in that moment and enveloped me in the Black of Knight, where I knew I would live, in the greatest of traditions, happily ever after.

THE SILENCE OF SWANS

Kannan Feng

There was a flash of white wings outside my window, and I knew that my brothers had returned.

Though I couldn't call to them, their appearance filled me with relief. They flew south over the winter, and as the days shaded warm again, I had begun to fear that they would not come back in time. I shuddered to think of coming to the end of my task only to find that my brothers were dead of a hunter's bolt or that they had finally given themselves over to live as swans forever.

My tower room was fragrant with the smell of asters, which the people of the palace call starwort. Five shirts lay completed in the cedar chest that sat at the foot of my bed, and the sixth was half-finished on the table. The king had been generous (too generous, the servants whisper) to the little ragbag he treed while on the hunt. The servants forgot that my not speaking didn't mean that I couldn't hear, and I knew how they felt about my mania for asters and the king's indulgence.

In less than a week's time, I would be able to stand up and throw six shirts woven of aster flowers over the heads of six swans, turning them back into my brothers. They would be men again, and I would be able to laugh and talk and sing the way that I used to. Our exiles were strangely alike except for all that they wore was feathers and I wore silk. All seven of us were without words, and sometimes I envied their shrieking calls to one another. I could make small sounds as well, but I had no companions with whom to communicate.

I waved through the window at them, and then I shut it. Swans have sharp eyes, and it was closing in on midnight.

He did not come every night, and even when he did, sometimes he only stood and watched me work over the shirts. He was the king of the land, and there were no doors that were barred to him. If he wished to watch a madwoman sew endlessly and silently with flowers, it was his right.

His name was Marek, but I had little enough cause to use it, and when he opened the door to my room, I stood and then knelt before him in greeting, a subject to her liege. Of course I did not speak.

He stripped his black leather gloves from his hands, and instead of telling me to rise, he came to stand close to me. He had bathed before the hunt. My nose was filled with the smell of sage soap, and underneath that was his own smell, warm and rich. He was a tall man, though not broad, and this close to him, I felt the way that I had when he first caught me. He could tear me to pieces if he wished, but something told me that he never would.

"Well, lovely," he said after a moment, "Do you think this will be the night that I make you speak?"

He spoke, and that gave me permission to raise my eyes to him. My expression of frank doubt and skepticism made him laugh, and he stroked a familiar hand down my cheek. I was the princess of a realm even greater than his, and it should have humiliated me when he petted me like a prize hunting dog. Instead, it filled me with warmth and pleasure, because I knew what was going to happen next.

He allowed me to put the delicate shirt that I was working on in the cedar chest, and he waited patiently while I loosened the laces of my kirtle. There were nights when he simply cut the laces with his knife, but tonight he seemed content to wait, sitting in my chair as I pulled away my heavy dress. He stayed still until I was down to my silk shift, and then he came to tug it over my head.

There was always a moment of delicious vulnerability when I was finally bare in front of him. My long black hair was still braided, failing to protect my modesty at all, and I left my hands at my sides, refusing to be cowed by his height or his strength. That made him laugh, and he took ruthless advantage of my confidence, stroking lean and calloused hands down the column of my neck, along my side and over my hips. His gentle touch made my nipples harden longingly, and he dipped his head to lick at one and then the other.

The heat and warmth of his tongue made me shift my weight from foot to foot. I knew that he was playing a game, and that there would be no easy climax for me that night, but I couldn't help the fact that my body craved him. Curse or not, I had wanted him since the moment I laid eyes on him, and he knew it.

"You're gorgeous, my little silent one," he murmured, moving to stand behind me. "Perfect in every part..."

He cupped my breasts, one in each hand. They were small, not even filling up the palms, but he regarded them as if they were precious. I gasped when he started to squeeze, digging his fingers gently into the soft flesh and making me crowd back against the hard bulk of his body. Standing so close, I could feel the length of his cock inside his trousers, and with a soft little cry, I pressed my rear against him.

Now, I could have moaned, *I'm ready now, can't you see?*

He laughed softly, kissing the rim of my ear, and one hand slid down my belly to the hair between my legs. His fingers were gentle but insistent, and when he found my clit there, he worked it until I was panting and red. I wasn't even pretending anymore. I pressed myself back against him, and if I could have, I would have turned to undress him. That didn't seem to be the game we were playing because he suddenly released me to stand away.

The loss of his body's warmth and support made me stumble, but then he closed both hands around my wrists and led me to the wall, turning me to face it. I wasn't sure what he was after until he placed my hands palm-flat on the stone.

"Don't move them from that spot," he whispered in my ear, and I nodded, swallowing hard.

He pressed one booted foot against my bare calf, and with a sigh, I braced my legs farther apart. The cool air hitting my damp parts made want more and more, and he laughed, dragging one hand up along my thigh to nestle between my legs.

I kept as still as I could as he pressed first one, then two fingers inside me. I was so wet that I took him easily, and for a blissful few moments, I worked myself on his hand, thinking that perhaps he would give me more. He drew his fingers away too soon, and he stepped away from me for a moment.

"Do you know what this is, lovely?"

I turned my head to see him holding what I at first mistook for a scourge, a short whip with a dozen knotted tails. The scourge was meant to punish criminals, and sometimes it could flay them to the bone. I must have gasped, because he laughed and stepped closer.

"Don't look so frightened, dear. This little toy is not meant to hurt you. I would never hurt you, do you understand that?"

I nodded immediately, and as a reward, he brought the falls of the strange thing to my cheek. The cords, which looked so frightening from a distance, were made of the softest doeskin, and I couldn't stop myself from pressing my face against them.

"This is meant to make you feel good, dearest. All you have to do is stay still."

With nothing else said, he came to stand behind me. I turned to face the stone, still nervous. Out of the corner of my eye, I could see the lazy swing of the toy in his hand, and when he brought it up, I couldn't stop myself from flinching.

Instead of striking me with it, however, he only ran the soft tails over my back, brushing them up and down so I could feel the drape of the leather across my skin. It was surprisingly sweet, and if I could have purred like a cat, I might have. I wondered if that was all; sometimes we played gently, and that brought as much pleasure as the nights when I had to bite down on my screams of pleasure.

The motion of the toy was hypnotic, and my body felt warm and hungry. There was something sleepy to it, and my eyes were just beginning to drift shut when he flicked the tails across my shoulders. That made me gasp and woke me up entirely, and I twisted my head to look at him.

"Turn back around, love," he said softly. "That was just the start."

I saw him cock back his arm as I turned back, and there wasn't enough time to brace myself before the tails caught me again between the shoulder blades. I shuddered. There was no sting, not really, but the weight of the tails was enough to bring a warmth to my flesh that hadn't been there before.

"You're going to love this," he promised, and then he struck me across the buttocks.

If the strokes across my shoulders had been warm, this sent hot pleasure stinging through my body. I closed my mouth around a whimper, and his hand landed on the curve of my rear, squeezing gently.

"Slide your hands farther down on the wall," he said. "Press your ass out toward me."

The commanding tone of his voice made me melt, and when I got myself into the position he indicated, I whimpered. This new position left my breasts hanging below me and my buttocks pushed out to him. I must have looked like a whore who was ready to be mounted, and all I wanted was a mirror so I could see myself like this.

He took his place behind me again, and this time there was no warning. He alternated blows left and right across my buttocks, striking harder and harder. I was breathing in time to his strokes, unsure whether I wanted to arch up against him or shy away. All I knew was that I needed to stay in position, and that there was nothing I needed to do beyond that. Giving myself up to him was a pleasure all its own.

I don't know how long I stood so still, but then there was a pause in the rain of blows and I wondered whether that meant that he would finally give me what I wanted. I was just turning my head to see what he was doing when he swept the lash low and caught me straight up between the legs.

I cried out and my hands dropped from the wall to press against the offended area. The sting was brief but so shocking, and I could feel how hot and wet I was. It made me blush hard, and that was before he grabbed my hands away roughly.

"On the wall," he said sternly. "Don't do that again."

I whimpered in response, and forced myself back to where I

had started. He made a displeased noise, and he pressed his foot against my calf again. I gasped in protest when I realized how widely he wanted my legs spread, but he was merciless. I pressed my hot face against the cold stone in front of me, whining in need and fear.

He drew out the wait until I was squirming, and then he landed another powerful blow between my legs. The tips of the tails caught me right on the slit, and I was certain one had snapped against the sensitive flesh of my clit. The sting and force of the blow made me wail, but this time, I maintained my position.

"Good girl, such a beautiful good girl," he purred, but his pleasure didn't stop him from landing another blow to the exact same spot and then another one after that. The sting built up even faster than it had on my rear, and I only realized that I was making a high wailing noise when my throat went dry.

I don't know how long he struck me like that, but when he stopped, I was drenched with sweat and out of my mind with desire. The delicious sting and soreness made me want so much more, and if I had had words, I might have begged him.

I heard him drape the toy over my table, and he came and drew me away from the wall to stand upright. Keeping both of my hands securely closed in one of his and twisted behind my back, he kissed me leisurely, exploring my mouth with his tongue when I was practically shaking apart with want. I wanted his fingers, his tongue, his cock, anything he could give me, and he was kissing me like we had all the time in the world.

He explored the hot flesh of my rear with his free hand, and he grinned at what he felt.

"I should keep you like this every day," he told me. "I could send a maid in to do it, would you like that? I could have her take you in hand before I come to see you, and then I would always find you just like this."

I thumped my head against his shoulder, utterly exhausted and needy. If it would have made him fuck me, if it would have gotten me what I wanted, I would have walked just as if I were in front of all the people of the palace.

He laughed softly, and I stifled a yelp when he bent me back into place.

No, no more! I thought, even as I knew I would love to be even hotter, to have yet more strokes between my legs.

He had different ideas, however, and to my relief, I heard him unbuckle his belt. He pressed his cock teasingly against the burning skin of my rear, and I wailed at him, telling him in no uncertain terms what I wanted. My breath caught when he pressed the tip of his cock against my rear hole. He had told me that he would fuck me that way some day, and I lived in dread and anticipation of it, but apparently he was just playing.

I felt him take his cock in hand and slide it straight inside me. I was so wet that there was no resistance at all, and I could feel the knuckles of his hand against one pained, raw cheek before he firmly grasped my hips.

Despite his calm, he was as ready as I was, and he practically bounced me off of his body, driving me toward the wall and making me press back against him. The metal of his belt dug into my abused flesh, and that was a pleasure itself.

He was talking less coherently now, telling me I was beautiful, telling me I was perfect, that he wanted me, that he loved me. The words rushed past my ears, and I wished I could respond to him. I wanted to tell him he was perfect, that I loved him, that I wanted nothing more than to please him and be pleased by him.

All I could do was show him what I meant with my body. I twisted up against him, bracing myself so he could fuck me harder, and crying out with the pleasure he gave me.

With a muffled swear, he bent forward and reached for my clit. He was rough with me, stopping just short of actually giving me pain, and it was exactly what I needed to crash right over the top. The climax shook me from the top of my head to the soles of my feet, and tears ran down my face with the intensity of it. I could feel my inner muscles clenching around him, and that brought him over too. He bit my shoulder when he finished, stifling his own cry.

For a long moment, he rested his weight on me, and we were simply still. The he steadied me with one hand on my hip and drew out of me gently. I sighed with the loss of him, feeling all over again how wet I was, and now the wetness on my thighs was joined by his seed as well.

He sat down on the chair and drew me to sit on his lap, simply holding me for a moment before reaching over for the pitcher of water. He wet a handkerchief and spreading my legs slightly, he started to clean me, ignoring the mess I was making of his trousers.

"You're crying," he said after a moment. "Did I hurt you?"

I smiled brightly at him, shaking my head. I draped my arms around his neck and planted a firm kiss on his lips. He laughed at me, but there was a wistful edge to it.

"Some day, perhaps you'll tell me what your name is," he said, and there was such a genuine sadness to it that I kissed him again.

Soon, I thought. The shirts were almost done, and soon I would be able to tell my lover exactly what he meant to me.

THE KING'S COUSIN

Catherine Paulssen

In a land faraway, a young princess played with her older sister's pearls. "I don't understand why you're marrying a man you've never met," she said.

"I have to do what is best for our people." Isabeau put another dress into a wooden box. "Our country isn't a very powerful nation. And you know the stories people tell about the king. He's a good man."

The young girl sighed dramatically. "But do you love him? Like our mother loved our father?"

Isabeau took a long look at the amulet she was wearing, which contained her parents' pictures. "Any woman is lucky to find love like that."

The little girl snatched the veil from a pile of folded clothes and draped it over her shoulders. Admiring her image in the mirror, she twirled around, catching rays of moonlight in her tight ringlets. "When I marry, I want to marry the handsomest prince of the three worlds!"

Her sister laughed. "And so you shall, little sister." She looked through the chamber she had occupied all twenty-two years of her life. "Now go, get some rest. We'll need to say good-bye by the rising of the sun."

After many days on the road, Isabeau reached the last leg of her journey. She traveled the remaining miles to the capital of the king's realm by boat. On her way west, she had passed giant mountains, forests that were endless and black, lakes that seemed bottomless. A shiver ran down Isabeau's spine as she thought of the dragons that were believed to dwell in dark holes in the shadows of the mountains.

"Look how welcoming everyone is," Persina, her old maid-servant, gently encouraged her. "And how they marvel at your bright golden hair! You will feel at home in no time."

Isabeau regarded the peasants, hunters and fishermen, the women and children who greeted them on both sides of the river, waving banners and lining the water with blossoms: their hair the color of bearskin, of raven feathers, their skin browned by the sun and calloused by the winds, and even the women standing head and shoulders above Isabeau, as strange to her as she was to them.

If the people had appeared tall and somehow sturdy to Isabeau, the king, who awaited her at a festively decorated landing stage, gave off the air of an oak tree. The midday sun sparkled in his wavy bister hair and against the huge, immaculate teeth of his welcoming smile.

His bulky appearance made the woman standing next to him seem even more slender. She held her head high and unlike the noble people behind her, she didn't cheer or wave; not even a smile made its way to her lips. She couldn't have been more than ten years her elder, but her opaque hair was already streaked with thin lines of silver, which gave it the shimmering color of mussels. A sparkling tiara was the one feature that lightened her appearance, which otherwise seemed to draw in the darkness of the surrounding pine trees and swallow all the shadows cast upon the square. Among the polished weapons of the guards, the glimmering golden flagpoles of the square, the sparkling eyes of the women who tossed white petals into the air, amongst the dancers, jesters and musicians, she didn't seem to belong.

"My dear Princess Isabeau," said the king, taking her hand and kissing it. "Welcome. I hope my country will become a treasured home to you. Whatever I can do to achieve that aim shall be done." Isabeau gave him her brightest smile, and the king introduced the stone-still woman next to him. "Lady Fallon, my cousin."

The woman curtsied to Isabeau, her eyes never leaving the princess's face. Bog oak eyes that could look right through a person, strip her to the bones—or so it felt to Isabeau. She tried to suppress a shiver that ran down her spine and held her hand out to Lady Fallon.

"I hope that we will be as close as sisters," she said with all the warmth she could muster.

Fallon didn't move, and blood rushed to Isabeau's cheeks at the thought of how much embarrassment it would cause her if the king's cousin would not return her gesture. Then, without saying a word, Fallon enclosed her slender fingers around Isabeau's. Her touch was chilly, and yet it seemed to Isabeau to sting like a hot iron. Fallon pulled the princess's hand closer to her face and pressed a fleeting kiss upon the coral ring she wore on her finger.

Isabeau forced a smile.

"You have to forgive my cousin," the king said with a broad

smile as he offered her his arm and made to move to his carriage. "She has been raised by sylphs; her only friend is her stallion, and her only love is her country."

Isabeau threw a glance back over her shoulder. Fallon must have heard every word. Did she see hurt flashing underneath the defiance in the woman's eyes? She turned back to the king and whispered, "Really, did sylphs raise her?"

The king laughed. "Legend has it. She can move as imperceptible to humans as the spirits of the air. My father took her to our castle when she was eight. She's my most trusted adviser; her auguries never fail. Of course, you will take her place now as the first lady of the kingdom."

After a deep and dreamless sleep, Isabeau needed some moments to remind herself where she was. She didn't have much time to contemplate, for a knock on her door, followed by the entry of a string of maidens, turned her mind to the preparations for the wedding celebration that would start that evening and last three days.

Isabeau soon felt at ease with her new maids who busied themselves preparing a perfumed bath and combing her hair, giggling good-naturedly at the way the kinked curls kept bouncing back. Persina was just helping her undress when the door opened without any warning or even a knock. Isabeau spun around, quickly covering her bare chest with her arms. "Lady Fallon!"

The maids stopped what they were doing, bowed their heads and made curtsies. "It is tradition that the female kin closest to the king have the privilege of preparing the bride for the ceremony," Fallon explained. At the slightest nod of her head, the maids quickly scurried out of the room—all but Persina, who stood by her mistress.

Isabeau straightened herself up. "I thank you, Lady Fallon, but I have my maid to help me," she said, trying to put as much dignity into her words as possible given that she was half naked.

"Do you want to insult me?" the lady demanded.

Isabeau blushed. "Of course not!"

"Leave," Fallon commanded Persina. With a reassuring look toward her mistress, who nodded shortly, the maid vanished.

"Persina," Isabeau began, "has been with me since the day I was—"

"Undress," Fallon said, her tone almost as sharp as when she had addressed the servants.

Isabeau felt her cheeks grow hot. She squinted her eyes and looked straight into the other woman's face, but it was a battle she was bound to lose. After several moments of tense silence, she gave in and stepped out of the nightgown that hung loosely around her waist. Fallon's eyes glided over her body and eventually, she reached for the pendant that dangled from Isabeau's neck on a golden chain. She opened it and studied the portrait inside.

"Your parents?" she asked and turned her eyes back to Isabeau's face.

The princess nodded, yanked the amulet out of the strange woman's hand, closed it and carefully placed it on the small table next to her. She felt completely bare now.

Without a word, she stepped into the steaming water, glad that it at least partially covered her.

To her surprise, Fallon knelt down next to the tub and grabbed a sponge, which she proceeded to dip into the water and then run over Isabeau's back. The hot water would have relaxed the princess had it not been for Fallon's presence. To distract herself from the strangeness of the situation, she focused on a string of black pearls that adorned the lady's slim neck and plunged into the deep well of her cleavage. "Did you know your parents?" she asked shyly.

"No," Fallon said shortly. She reached around Isabeau and began stroking her upper body with the sponge. Her wrist brushed against Isabeau's skin, leaving warm sizzles in its wake. Fallon's slender hands touched her in a way Persina's never had. They aroused sensations unknown and so overwhelming she wondered if they were conjured up by her imagination or maybe even without her will. She remembered the king's words about Fallon's upbringing, and the way the woman's hands flew over her skin, the lightness and delicacy of her touch, convinced her that the king's cousin must indeed be the offspring of invisible fairies.

Driven by curiosity and something hidden very deep inside her, a feeling she couldn't name, Isabeau arched her back. As if she had been expecting this, Fallon tended to the round breasts that now poked out of the water. Her bathing felt like a caress. Isabeau's nipples hardened, and for a moment, she wondered how it would feel if it were her fingers instead of the sponge circling her skin. The sheer thought and the fear that Fallon could read it made her want to die in shame. She peeked at Fallon's face, but the onyx surface of her eyes remained unperturbed. Nevertheless, Isabeau tried to hide her enlarged nipples as inconspicuously as possible.

Fallon paused for a moment and looked straight into the princess's eyes. Without a word, she reached for Isabeau's arms and spread them. Her breasts jutted out of the water now, and the nipples contracted when they hit the cold air. Isabeau could feel Fallon's gaze on them and tried to concentrate instead on the drops of water splattering on the surface of the floor. She reminded herself that this woman had reason to dislike her and had treated her with nothing but rudeness so far. And yet it was impossible to silence the turmoil inside her body.

At last, Fallon got up and unfolded a large linen cloth, which she wrapped around Isabeau. Once more, she got on her knees and rubbed the cloth up and down the princess's legs. A jolt of electricity zapped through Isabeau's body when suddenly, Lady Fallon cupped the delta between her legs and, with soft pressure, pressed the palm of her hand against the softened hairs and lips.

"You will give birth," she said, and her breath brushed against Isabeau's thighs. "But there's not much time." She slowly withdrew her fingers. Isabeau's knees gave in, and she stumbled.

"I can do the rest by myself," she said. "Thank you."

Fallon got up. She put her hand underneath Isabeau's chin and raised her head. Isabeau was so close she could taste her breath, and it smelled of wild honey. For a moment, she was sure the other woman would kiss her, and yet Fallon didn't move. Instead, her eyes flickered for a moment before she nodded and with a last look, vanished swiftly and without a sound but the rustling of the feathers that adorned the rim of her dress.

Isabeau turned her eyes to the mirror and ran her fingers over her mouth. Her hand slid down between her legs, and she could feel the wetness that wasn't caused by the bath. Had she fallen under a spell? Was it dark magic that Fallon had used to bewitch her? Whatever power it was that the woman wielded over her, it had seemed like the perfect way to humiliate her.

And yet it somehow hadn't.

It was only after silence had fallen over the castle and an ashen moon was casting its beams on her bed that the king visited Isabeau's chamber. She had never been with a man; however, she had heard her share, caught the bashful accounts maids whispered to each other across the castle grounds about what men did when they lay with a woman.

The king made his best effort to please her before he thrust his hips against hers and entered her in a moment whose pain she could still feel the next day. As he thrashed above her, panting and kneading her breasts, she couldn't help but think of Fallon, who had stroked her body so gently that the memory of her touch still made Isabeau blush. She took it as another sign of the woman's mysterious magic that reliving the sensation made her sizzle rather deliciously.

A few days after the wedding, the king left for the North with his most trusted knights, leaving the government in the hands of his council—and his cousin. Rumors had reached the capital of a secret alliance near the country's borders, and the small army set out to defeat the enemies before they could unite and reach the kingdom. From the castle's highest tower, Isabeau watched him and his retinue leave. Will-o'-the-wisps danced over the marshes in the distance. In the stables, the barn owls screeched.

When word arrived that her husband had been killed on the battlefield, Isabeau did not feel overcome with the grief she thought befitting a widowed queen. Instead, worry filled her heart. Would the noblemen accept her as the ruler without a husband at her side? Would Lady Fallon?

Isabeau recalled the words she had spoken after bathing her and finally understood their meaning. But until she was certain that she'd be giving the mourning kingdom an heir to the throne, she would have to find other ways to make herself indispensable. In the king's absence, it had become obvious to her that she would never be able to outdo Fallon in the realm of politics. So Isabeau removed most of her jewelry and slipped into a simpler dress. She would use the weapons she possessed in abundance: her beauty, her exoticness and the popularity she enjoyed among the peasants. Her walks through the capital's streets soon became a much-anticipated event among the poor and sick.

When she returned to the castle after one of her strolls, Persina greeted her with a solemn face. She told her of a secret message she had received, how ogres had united with the wild people across the sea to attack the land she had called home until lately.

Isabeau's face grew pale at the thought of the monstrous barbarians, descendants of giants. "And ogres…they feed on the flesh of children and virgins," she whispered.

"You have to find a way to send aid," Persina urged her.

Isabeau shook off the vision of the castle where her little sister was living invaded by hideous creatures. "The king only took the knights closest to him. There are still plenty of warriors on standby."

The women jerked around when the door creaked and fell into the hatch. Persina went outside, but the passageway was empty.

"It was only the wind," said Isabeau to calm the elderly maid as well as her own nerves. "Leave now and send word to my sister that I'll see to her and our people's protection."

By early morning, she had perfected her plan. She knew that if she told the council the full truth, they would never send knights that far away but instead double the forces protecting their nearest borders. She was confident, however, that she could sweet-talk the old men of the council into doing what she wanted: Maybe they would even welcome the opportunity to break Lady Fallon's grip over them by siding with her. She waited until the lady's horse was saddled and bridled for her daily ride through the woods before summoning the council.

"We need to be prepared for all eventualities," she told the old men. "The troops will protect our extended borders and by doing so guarantee the safety of all of our people."

"She's not telling the truth!" an angry voice shouted behind her. Isabeau spun around. How had she failed to notice Fallon's entrance?

"She knows that the ogres are uniting with forces across the sea!" Fallon cast an imperial glance over the men in the round. "If you grant her request, you will send our warriors to a certain death!"

Hot shudders ran down Isabeau's back. How did she know? How could she have found out?

A few of the men sneered. "The ogres with the barbarians across the sea? Everyone knows they've been enemies for centuries!"

Isabeau quickly wiped her damp palms against her belly. "You noblemen know that I have dedicated myself to the well-being of our late king's subjects." With a sly smile, she stepped in front of the window, knowing that the red light of the late sun would give her frizzy hair the look of a glowing torch. "And so I demand you grant my wish in the name of the unborn heir to the king's throne," she said with a steady voice that belied the pounding of her heart.

Murmurs ran through the rows. "Queen Isabeau is well respected among the people," the oldest of the politicians eventually said.

"The East is our only passage to the sea," another contributed.

Fallon's eyes were fixed on the queen like Devil's Berries in a pale face, burning into her skull, incandescent with fury as the men finally assented to Isabeau's request.

It didn't matter at all to Isabeau. She had gotten what she came for. She thanked the noblemen, bowed her head and made for the door. When she brushed past Fallon, she couldn't keep from shooting her a triumphant look.

"You will regret your deceit," the dark woman said, only for her to hear.

Isabeau stopped. "I don't think this prophecy of yours will come true," she answered haughtily.

Fallon tilted her head. "You have your means," she said, her eyes gliding over Isabeau's figure. "And I have mine."

In the evening, Isabeau was still so giddy from achieving victory that not even Fallon's threat could extinguish her high. She took a sip from the wine Persina had brought her and looked outside her window to the east. Gloaming mists wafted over the country, and even her chamber was filled with a chilly, unnatural aura. Yet before she could so much as fathom the eerie presence, she was overcome with fatigue. She quickly slipped underneath the blankets and drifted into dreams in which a faceless, even bodiless person caressed her. The shadow spoiled her with what seemed like more than just one pair of hands. They ran along her sides, traced up her arms and tickled her wrists. She wiggled her body and found that the hands had become heavy, pressing her into the cushions. The pressure felt so real that she woke up with a gasp.

Half asleep, she tried to sit up and shake off the dream. The drowsiness vanished all at once when she found her wrists tied to the bedposts. Beyond that, there was a weight on her hips and a terrifying grip clasping her thighs. She was about to scream, but her eyes widened in horror as a hand was pressed onto her mouth. A rustling sound froze the blood in her veins and then, out of thin air, a face appeared, hovering above her.

"Lady Fallon," she whispered under the firm hand silencing her.

"I will let go, but if you make any noise that alerts someone, I will hurt whoever enters this room. Do you understand?"

She swallowed hard, but nodded. Fallon removed her hand, and Isabeau gulped for air. "How...how do you—" she stammered, but her words died in her throat as the rest of Fallon's body became slowly visible and her question was answered. "You own an invisible coat!" she cried. "So that's how..." Everything became clear to her now. The auguries. The silence with which Fallon moved. The sudden appearances.

"...how I got behind your little plotting."

"Let me go," demanded Isabeau. She tried to wriggle, but Fallon had her thighs firmly pressed to the bed with the strength of her legs. "I'm just trying to protect my country."

"So am I," Fallon said calmly. "And I will not let you impose upon its people for your own purposes."

"You can't hold me in here forever."

Fallon simply laughed. "You don't know what I'm able to do in order to force your hand."

"I'm your queen!" Isabeau hissed.

"No, you're not," Fallon spat. "Nothing gives you supremacy over me. And there's already word that your marriage to my cousin was never consummated."

Isabeau's eyes shot daggers. "You! You did that. Oh, you..." She struggled to get the woman off of her. "You know I'm with child!"

Fallon smiled slyly. "One word from me, and your regency will never be questioned." She pushed Isabeau's shoulders back into the pillows. "The councilmen fear me, but they also know where my loyalties are," she added sharply. "Now hush and listen. Tomorrow, you will summon the council and take your request back."

Isabeau shook her head. "I can't do that. I can't let my country go down like that."

"This is your country now."

Tears rimmed Isabeau's eyes. "My sister's still there. I can't."

"You have to."

Isabeau turned her eyes away from Fallon's probing stare and contemplated her options. "If you let me," she finally said, "I will issue a declaration in a couple of days telling the council that I have received word that what you said about barbarians and ogres uniting is true. I will then ask every able man who is willing to prove himself by standing up to fight them. Those that heed my call will not only be heroes but also serve their homeland because to protect the extended borders means to act in the interest of their own people. After all, once the enemies have conquered my father's land, they will have access to the country's rich supplies and stocks to get through the winter. They can gather their strength and attack with renewed force in the spring."

Fallon smiled. "You're a clever little witch."

Isabeau puckered her lips defiantly. "I was raised to become a queen."

For the first time, she detected something resembling respect in Fallon's eyes. The two women stared at each other for some long moments. Then Fallon ran her finger over Isabeau's heaving chest, and her eyes took in the nipples that grew hard beneath the nightgown.

"You don't have to be afraid of me anymore," she said, her voice softer than Isabeau had ever heard it.

She licked her dry lips. "I'm not."

Fallon's eyes flashed. She reached underneath her robe and produced a small dagger. Expecting to be cut loose, Isabeau stiffened when instead, the blade was placed right below her collarbone. She held her breath as it moved down the length of her body, the pointy tip breaking through her gown and trailing along her skin. Fallon's composed bearing was broken only by the glaring in her eyes, and the realization of just how much she was at the stronger woman's mercy made Isabeau's blood rush in agitation.

Fallon regarded the fair skin that emerged underneath the cut gown and parted the folds with a brush of her fingers. Isabeau shivered as her breasts were almost completely exposed to the all-consuming eyes. She grew scared again, but the tingling between her legs made it impossible to deny the thrill that mixed with her fear.

Fallon's finger traced the chain of the amulet resting between Isabeau's breasts. Her palm ran over the golden oval. "I know that you're looking for what your parents had," she whispered. In a move Isabeau hadn't expected, she bent down and kissed her. Dazzled by the sudden force, she was too taken aback to return the gesture of affection.

"But you hate me!"

"No." Fallon swallowed, and her breath caressed Isabeau's mouth. "I don't."

This time, Isabeau kissed her back.

Afterward, her eyes turned back to the ties that bound her to the bed. Fallon saw the silent request and smirked. "It's not time for you to be freed yet."

"I won't beg," Isabeau said and writhed against the bands.

"Shh," Fallon whispered and stroked some curls off the queen's heated forehead. "Stop fighting it." She placed little kisses on Isabeau's face.

"Did you poison my wine?" Isabeau asked, a sudden notion alarming her. Every fiber in her body wanted to give in, but her mind couldn't let go.

Fallon laughed. "Mandrake and valerian." She ran her finger along Isabeau's arm. "You looked so innocent in your sleep that I almost forgot what I came for."

Isabeau wanted to tell her exactly what she thought about this witchery, but all thoughts cleared from her mind when Fallon cupped her bare breasts. She massaged the nipples with her thumbs and soon they were puffy and so darkly pink Isabeau thought they were literally begging for Fallon's attention. Instead Fallon abandoned them to kiss her navel, licking at the small hollow as though she were drinking from it. Her caress stirred a small flame in Isabeau's belly that zinged right between her legs. She writhed underneath the woman's touch and moaned with satisfaction when Fallon finally kissed the spot between her breasts. Her tresses softly stroked Isabeau's trembling flesh, her nose caressed the curves of the young queen's body and muffled sighs escaped her mouth as she explored them with her hands, nostrils and lips.

Isabeau gasped as Fallon finally teased her nipple with the tip of her tongue. She sunk deep into the pillows, biting her lips to suppress the heavy moans that rose from depths hidden so deep inside her she wondered how Fallon could have uncovered them. Suddenly, Fallon pulled back from the rosy tip and grazed the other breast with her mouth. "You're cruel," Isabeau panted. With a slowness so deliberate it seemed intended to prove Isabeau's words and at the same time punish her for them, Fallon let one hand wander down between her legs and started to circle her soft, throbbing heat. The vibrations it sent through Isabeau's body vanquished all other sensations and filled her with a new bliss: pleasures so unbearably high, so tantalizingly unfulfilled.

"Is that...is that still the effect of the potion?"

Soft laughter purled against her stomach. Isabeau stretched her neck to catch a glimpse of the woman's head buried between her thighs. A groan escaped her lips as Fallon's pointed tongue darted against her, again and again. Isabeau clenched her teeth to suppress any moans that would alarm Persina, a task that became more and more impossible as Fallon began to suck her. She caved in to the rhythm the other woman's tongue dictated. The bed creaked as she bucked against the bonds that held her in place. Fallon pressed a firm hand on her hips, but even she was powerless against the force of the waves that gripped Isabeau's body and shook her wildly, sending her into golden, blinding heights. She continued to caress her until the last ripples of ecstasy had ebbed away, leaving Isabeau sighing, whispering, panting her lover's name.

With a few quick moves of her dagger, Fallon cut the bands holding the queen in place. A small drop of sweat ran down her neckline, and Isabeau could taste the impatience on her tongue, urging her to follow its trail. She sat up and brushed a strand of Fallon's hair out of her face.

"What will we do now?" she asked.

"By day, you're queen," Fallon said, nudging Isabeau's mouth with her lips. "But at night, you're mine."

NEED AND PERMISSION

Benjamin Creek

Milady?"

The footman's voice was low. Marienne sighed and set down her quill.

"Dinner is served, milady. He's waiting for you."

His message delivered, the servant vanished. Marienne leaned back in her chair, looking at the pages of her diary fluttering in the wind. The candles on her desk guttered in the freshening breeze, sending shadows flickering across her words.

It seemed like she'd been writing the same things over and over, going back months now. Stroking the paper, she walked back through her past thoughts. She had set aside her commonplace book an hour before, finished with the mundane details of the vast estate she now managed. *This* book was significantly more private, locked and bound in brass and leather.

Those words gave her a pleasant shiver that faded into the sinking feeling that was becoming so dully, painfully familiar. She pressed her lips together, thinking about her husband.

Andray was doubtless immaculately dressed, seated at one side of the table—he had told her once he did not want to sit at the head of the table, but at her side. He would be waiting patiently, not even sipping his wine; when she entered, he would smile and stand, seat her, exchange words as interesting as the ledgers and household notes in her commonplace books.

There wasn't much beast in him, not anymore. He carried himself as if he was terrified he would hurt her, physically or emotionally. There was still the deep, smoky heat in his eyes, the banked fires that had burned into her heart when she had first met him. But when he touched her, when they made love, he did not seem to understand that he no longer had to restrain the bestial strength that had fascinated her so much.

The claws and fur and terrible horns were all gone, banished by her love and her acceptance, but he bore a strange and painful diffidence inside him now, and he touched her with reluctance, fearing to cause pain. When they went to be together, he was attentive, always giving her pleasure first. But he either refused or was unable to understand that Marienne needed something more than that.

Her desk was stacked with books written by strong women, women she had grown to respect and admire as she read their words, women who spoke lovingly, sensually, of the unbridled joy of submission. Each had given herself to her lover, to be toyed with and used; each had been bound and beaten, even branded, and each in her own way had attained a soaring fulfilment and a strange new freedom.

Marienne's fingernails dug into her palms. She wanted so desperately for Andray to grip her tight, throw her down and make her feel the heat of his desire for her. She wanted to give him everything she had, to break down the walls of fear that he had built up inside over the years of his curse, but they were too strong, and she could not bring herself to force it. In so many ways, he was so fragile.

So, she wrote. Every time his grip started to tighten on her arm and he jerked away as if stung; every time his teeth closed around her neck, only to snap open, leaving her with a muttered apology that instantly curdled the seething heat in her belly, she wrote. Her desires poured out onto the page, and as she elaborated in secret on what she needed from her husband, she grew more and more dissatisfied with the reality.

She pushed herself away and stood, trying to prepare herself mentally for dinner. She was going to get an apology for calling her away from her books, when she would have preferred a spanking for being late, and she was just going to have to try to accept it.

Andray stood when she entered, just as she had known he would; he smiled and apologized, and she gave a brittle smile back. They ate in heavy silence, and she remembered the ridiculous thrill she used to get, watching him devour the rare red meat his body had required. There was something about those teeth that made her pulse speed up. Even now, he pulled his lips back as he bit savagely into a piece of bread—an unconscious habit from the past—and she felt herself moistening.

She bent toward him, lips parted, and he looked up uncertainly. "I'm sorry, my dear," he said quietly, setting the bread down. "I forgot myself."

Sigh. Gone again. She stood up. "I am not hungry, Andray," she said, bitterness seeping into her voice. "I believe I will go for a walk in the gardens."

He perked up at that; he loved his gardens, as he loved anything that gave her happiness, but she swept away before he could offer to join her, leaving him standing awkward and confused at the table.

The cool air of the evening didn't help. Marienne crossed her arms and wished she'd brought a shawl, or a glass of brandy, but there was no help for it. The exercise was pleasant, anyway. And it was wonderful to see the care her husband lavished on his flowers. The gardens were laid out with masterful precision.

She stopped by a sapling and fingered the twine that held it upright until it grew strong. Peering at the knot, she felt her heart swell at the skill with which it had been tied, imagining Andray's strong fingers looping silk around her wrists. Shivering from more than the chill breeze, she quickened her steps back to her room and her writing desk to scrawl her fantasies out until she was exhausted.

Her shoes clicked along tile as she neared her room, and she frowned; there were no servants about, and her door hung open. That was strange. Lamplight spilled out, which was even stranger; she never left a fire going by her precious books.

When she pushed through the door, she stopped with a jerk, staring. The chair of her writing desk was pushed back, and it was occupied. Andray sat, his chin sunk in his right hand; the laces of his white silk shirt were undone, and his left hand held her diary, resting on his thigh.

Quick anger surged in her at the invasion of her privacy, only to be banished in moments by a wild spike of hope. Marienne felt her blood running red hot and a flush mounting to her pretty cheeks. Next to the book through his trousers she could see the heavy curve of her husband's erection.

He looked up, and she could see the coals turning to real fire inside his eyes. He lifted the book. "This is truly how you feel?" he said, his voice low and dark.

She was balanced on a wire, and she made her decision instantly.

"Yes, lord."

"Take off your dress."

There was a calm certainty in his command that made her heart leap and her fingertips fly to her buttons. She almost giggled when she realized that she was shaking too hard to quickly undo them, and then he was standing in front of her, his hands closed around hers, and she was more aroused than she had been since he had transformed. Thread snapped and buttons popped as he slowly, inexorably ripped the fabric from her body.

It was only moments, but it felt like minutes stretching into hours as her husband tore her covering away, leaving her standing proud in her shift, her nipples pointing stiff and tingling through the thin cloth.

"You were late to dinner tonight." The calmness he had affected at first was strangled by lust, his voice thick in his throat.

"It won't happen again, my lord," she said, and the soft submission she wanted to show was ruined by her spiking desire; her voice cracked in the middle of her sentence, and Andray's face broke into the broadest, most genuine grin she'd ever seen on him.

"Get on your knees, Marienne," he growled, and she obeyed gladly.

"Put your hands behind your back."

Her wrists crossed each other at the small of her back, and she felt a wicked anticipation in her belly at the barely restrained arousal in her husband's words.

He trembled as he fumbled at his trouser strings, and she bent in to kiss his fingers. He curled his hands into her long, black hair, and she slowly undid his pants with her teeth. She could feel his cock hard against her cheek through the cloth, and she thought she was going to die of the tension before she got it free.

Then, the knot was undone, and Andray sucked in a breath

as his erect phallus rose before his wife's eyes. He couldn't speak, so he motioned to her, and she captured his gaze as she leaned in close to suck the tip of him into her mouth.

Maybe it was the literature and the long fantasies that had primed her for this moment, but Marienne had never felt quite so *alive*, so free and powerful and *herself* as she did just then, on her knees before her husband, his cock hot and hard inside her mouth. She heard his moan, felt the way his fingers tightened in her hair, and her heart jumped.

He had never asked her to do this, and she could never bring herself to broach the subject. And now that it was finally happening, she was somewhat at a loss. Tentatively, she tried to take more of his length past her lips, but it wasn't too many inches before her insuppressible gagging stopped her. Steeling herself, she focused her attention on his cockhead, and the shocked sound that came from his mouth when she sucked hard on him, her tongue flat against the bottom of his hardness, made her feel triumphant.

When she met his eyes again, he was looking at her like he'd never seen her before. She squealed happily as he scooped her up in his arms, kissing her fiercely, their tongues tangling in each other's mouths as their bodies pressed close together. She rolled her hips, pressing herself against his leg, and he threw her backward onto the bed.

She lay on her back, her body twisting with the wild desire that bubbled inside her, and she raised her arms so he could strip her nude. Her shift joined his shirt on the floor, and he kicked clumsily out of his trousers, hampered by his utter inability to stop looking at her lovely nakedness.

When he bent over her, she wrapped her arms around his neck, but he brushed them away. "No, Marienne," he said, holding a sash in front of her eyes. "Give me your hands."

Her heart thudded in her throat as her husband tied her wrists together, the knots skillful as she had fantasized, and she gasped softly when he pushed her down again, spreading her legs. She had a moment only to realize what he was doing, and then his tongue was inside her, his lips hot on her clitoris, and her body arched as a long finger penetrated her.

Delirious, she babbled his name, wriggling on the bed as he pleasured her relentlessly. Her bound hands pulled his head closer against her, until he finally grabbed the sash, took her by the hips and flipped her over.

Instantly, she raised her rump toward him, and he caressed her, planting soft kisses in a line up the smooth curves of her back. He kissed her neck, and she sighed; then, his teeth bit into her skin and the sigh transformed into a whimper of delicious pain. He pulled her roughly against his body, and she felt his hard length against her soft flesh.

There was time, just enough time, to whisper his name once more, and then he was at her gates and inside her. Her breath left her with a shuddering sound as he filled her, one hand gripping her hip, the other at her neck. Her mouth fell open as he fucked her, stroking smoothly into her slick, hot center.

She felt wholly present, felt like she was entirely together with her lover, and when a long arm snaked around her waist to press hard against her swollen clit, just as he slid deep inside her once more, her body shivered as her orgasm came like stumbling off a cliff into a sea of purple-red haze.

It rose and rose inside her as her husband kept fucking her, and she moaned raggedly, squeezing down to feel the wonderful hardness of him more fully. He growled, his nails marking her hips as he abandoned finesse to take her as she wanted to be taken. She cried out her glee as he used her bestially, plowing her until it almost hurt.

The sharp pleasure of it made her eyes water, and she felt his breath on her hair as he sped up. "I love you," he breathed, and her eyes opened wide as his cock twitched, buried deep inside her, and suddenly filled her belly with his seed.

Her momentarily quiescent climax suddenly spiked again, and she laughed with sheer happiness as her husband stood still, his prick still spurting liquid heat into her. She could hear his breathing slow and steady as he recovered and shrank, and then she wormed her hands out of the binding sash and wriggled around to see him.

Her face shone, and there was a deep adoration in his eyes as he looked down at her. Sinking into the bed, he lay beside her, husband and wife together, and they rested in the shared sweetness of each other's company, regaining their strength.

Marienne nestled her head into Andray's shoulder, while feeling the tiny red streaks where his teeth and nails had marked her. She kissed his chest, and he laughed softly.

"I love you, husband," she said, rising to her feet, and he smiled like daybreak as she stretched, her body glowing. Her own grin joined his and lit up the room. "But next time, I don't want to be able to walk afterward."

LOCKS

Tahira Iqbal

The thousand-dollar-a-plate benefit is amazing. The cause, close to my father's heart, ensures that he digs deep into his wallet at the auction, which is already in the seven figures. Amazing.

But I'm on edge. Utterly on edge.

"I'm just going to the bathroom," I say, leaning across while the bidding heats up for a Matisse.

"Okay," he says, before nodding to a group of men at the side of the room.

"Father..." I whisper pleadingly in his ear.

"Cara, security will go where you go."

The guests at the table are all looking at me, so I smile and pick up my purse. The men at the table rise, tipping their heads briefly as I depart. I keep the smile going, weaving through the tables. The red Prada dress—one shoulder, to the floor—captures attention. Cameras go off, women whisper. But I know it's my hair they are really interested in as it snakes around my waist, feeling just as jittery as I am.

In the safety of the empty bathroom, cleared by the security team, I pat the wheat-blonde belt that's constricting like a snake. Tears rise. But I don't let them fall. I won't ever let them fall, even as I recall last week.

That man...with a knife in one hand and a fist full of my hair in the other.

There's a knock at the door. I jump out of my skin and my hair drops to the back of my knees. It nearly touched the floor last week.

"Ma'am?"

"I'm coming." I smile at the woman in the mirror.

It doesn't stick.

I exit, walking with the security team back toward the ballroom. There's a commotion behind me; noise, like a door being forcefully opened. Then a gunshot. Someone to my left falls. More shots. I'm dragged bodily out of the way, into a corridor. My knees tremble as I press my hands over my ears.

The man holding me back whispers hotly into his cuff before looking at me. "North exit. Go. Someone will meet you there."

"What about you?"

His eyes go to steel. "It was an honor serving you, Princess. And your mother when she was alive."

There's a single figure coming round the corner...not one of the bodyguards. It's him...the man who attacked me last week.

"Go!"

I run as bullets tear through the corridor.

He wants me.

The descendant of Rapunzel. My hypnotic hair the focus of the deranged few who covet its potent power.

I crash through the emergency doors, finding myself on a loading bay.

I gasp. A man waits with a gun trained on the door that I've just flown through. He's dressed in a black suit, just like the men I'd left behind....

"Princess," He lowers the weapon immediately. "Andrew sent me."

I put my ass to the edge of the dock, but it's too far down to jump and I'm in heels.

"I've got you." His dark eyes, assured and comforting, meet mine. He puts his hands up, and they connect with my waist. I slide down the dock wall and against his body.

We go tearing into the night in the SUV.

A cell rings; he presses a button on the wheel.

"Logan, talk to me," comes a deep voice; it's the head of security, Andrew.

"I have the Diamond."

"You know what to do." And the call ends.

I blink back the tears, watching the signs on the highway drift by.

"We're not going to the palace?"

"I'm taking you out of the city."

I hold my breath as another sign flies by denoting that we're entering a new county. "Please tell me you're not taking me to the estate?"

Logan doesn't answer me.

We park on the circular drive an hour later, bile involuntarily rising in my throat. When I see Jess, my assistant, once my nanny, standing at the open door looking as nervous as I feel, I exit the car and fling myself into her arms.

"It's all right, miss. I've done my best to make this home. Mr. Smith was quite insistent on your safety," says the middle-aged woman.

"Let's get inside." Logan scans the dark landscape around

us, nodding to the patrol at the door. I'd seen at least four others when we'd pulled up. And the guards on the gate had guns resting across their chests, fingers poised against the triggers.

I stare up at the high ceiling, the hallway bright, lit by the bulbous chandelier that my father had shipped from Italy. I swallow back my fear, but it's no use, my blood is cold, my mind numb. Some of the furniture still has dust sheets over it.

I close my eyes. "Is my room ready, Jess?"

"Yes, miss."

Quickly, I head upstairs. It's warm, set for my stay, and the curtains have been drawn. I stare down at the dress... There are splashes of blood on the base of it. I haul the side zip down, panting as I do, before tearing out of it and kicking it away.

The door opens.

I face Logan in my underwear. "Don't you know how to knock?"

He's not looking at my body. His eyes immediately drop to the bruises across my right hip and ribs. Logan closes the gap between us, causing my heart to kick-start again.

My anger drains suddenly, leaving me exhausted. "There was blood on the dress...from..."

He shrugs out of his jacket, and I slip my arms into the sleeves. "I did some homework. Hair from the descendant of Rapunzel..." He whistles, "An ounce goes for thousands."

"Don't..." I hug the jacket tight around me; I can feel it graze the back of my thigh, just above the knee.

"I'm going to keep you safe, but I need you to get over the fear."

"I'm not afraid."

"Your hands are telling me a different story."

I stare down at my trembling fingers.

"You need to be strong in order to get through this."

I look up at him, angry. He has no idea how strong I've had to be.

"Get some sleep." He rises. "I'll be downstairs."

I wake at dawn, changing into my own clothes, which were placed in the guest closet down the hall so that I wouldn't be disturbed. Jess has set breakfast in the kitchen. Her smile is as tight as mine, her moves clipped and sharp. "Jess," I say, taking her hand once she's poured me a tea. "It's not for long."

"I don't like you being here, miss. Too many bad memories."

My nerves tingle as I think about her words. The meaning of them. Of being here. "Where's Logan?"

"Mr. Smith said something about walking the perimeter—" I rise and she says quickly, "Miss, he asked for you to stay inside!"

But I'm already walking out.

I find him on the drive, walking toward the house, on his cell. His every muscle tenses as he sets his sights on me. His black, cropped hair catches the early morning light.

"I'll call you back, Andrew." He puts the phone into the pocket of his padded jacket, "You need to stay inside."

"Take me back to the city."

His eyes are rimmed with tiredness, but he's hiding it well. His navy tee looks fresh and his jeans cover long, muscular legs.

"Did you hear me? I want to go back to the palace."

"No."

I inhale roughly. "You can't keep me here."

"Yes I can."

I'm about to say something acidic, when the breath is knocked out of me. I double over, hands to my knees.

"What's wrong?" Logan's beside me, as are the others who are stationed outside. My cry of alarm makes me buckle, but Logan doesn't let me fall. "Cara?"

"I'm okay..." But I'm barely able to catch my breath.

"You don't look it."

I know what I must look like, and I blush. Sweat starts to bead as I begin to pant.

"I'll get a doctor."

"No..." I moan. "It's... I'm not sick...just get me inside."

He does as I ask, whisking me to my bedroom, in his arms. I fight the urge to bury my face against his chest.

"What is it?" He sets me on my feet.

"They're using." I gingerly walk to the bed.

"Using what?"

"My hair... Oh!" My back arches as I begin to tremble.

"Your hair...?"

I bite my lip, but I'm not able to stop the moan as I pitch forward, fisting the sheets.

"Oh..." His voice is raw. "Are you...?"

A long, protracted moan of dislocated desire rockets through me as I come.

I sink to the floor, noting that Logan has gone. Something inside flickers with hurt until he strides back from the closet with a blanket that he drapes over me.

I hug it close, leaning against the bed frame, aching. God, I've soaked through my panties.

Logan's face remains impassive as he crouches beside me. "So it's true...your hair is used in sex rituals."

I nod, embarrassed to the high heavens and wasted from the exertion of it all.

"And you feel it...even though it's not part of you anymore?"

I nod again, utterly breathless.

"Holy shit."

"Can you help me up?"

He does so. "Do you need to…rest?"

"I need a shower."

"Your father never told me this."

"How could he tell you?" I say, putting my hand on the en suite door handle, "Oh, by the way, my daughter has an orgasm when her hair is used in magic?"

"Point taken."

I palm my forehead. "You're wondering what the hell you've got yourself into aren't you?"

"No. I'm wondering how to find the guys that did this to you." He pulls out his cell and leaves.

I spend the day in my room, eating lunch and dinner there, and don't see Logan until I get up in the middle of the night, thirsty.

"You're awake?"

I turn, startled. It's Logan, standing by his bedroom door fully dressed.

"I wanted something to drink."

We take a seat at the breakfast bar. Logan's made a coffee that could wake the dead, while I sip an herbal tea.

"She died here," I say, quietly, staring at the table.

"I know."

"And you still brought me here?"

"It's secluded, totally secure. Perfect."

"They got to my mom here…"

"I'm not going to let anything happen to you."

I get images of Logan's hand tracing down my back when he'd taken care of me earlier. His breathing had become altered…the distinct flush of arousal staining his cheeks, his pupils blown.

"Cara?"

"I have to go..." There's a forceful cramp settling in my lower belly. I swiftly exit and run two at a time up the stairs and make it in time to my bed just as the orgasm hits.

Jess meets me at the bottom of the stairs the next morning, "Are you all right?"

I nod, trying to adjust my stance. But everything *hurts*. I was taken four times.

After breakfast, I find Logan; he's been walking the grounds again. He takes off his parka, draping it over the back of a chair in the den where I am.

"They got you? Again?" I pull my collar up, hoping to hide the hickeys. "Answer me Cara."

"I'm fine." I get off the couch, aim for the door.

"You keep saying that." He bars my progress and tips my chin up with his fingers so that he can look me right in the eye.

I pull myself away. Heading back to my room, the tension is exploding within. I find my handbag, then the keys to the Maserati that Father keeps here. I nearly mow down two of the bodyguards and destroy the wooden barrier as I hurtle onto the main road.

Logan's SUV follows. Fast.

The car sticks to the curves of the road; I cross the miles with ease. My cell rings. I answer the unknown number.

"Pull over." Logan's voice is as dark as thunder. I disconnect the call, press the gas pedal harder. The cells rings again.

"Leave me alone, Logan."

"Pull the fucking car over now."

We're going nearly ninety miles an hour on a single track road. Someone's going to get killed. I do as he demands. I exit the car, slamming the door as hard as I can.

"You can't keep me there!" I jab my finger behind him.

The trace of anger is clear in his stride, boots heavy on the tarmac. "Get in the car."

I give him silence. Hard and heavy silence; my hair rising like a cobra, sizing him up.

We're on an isolated road, just the sounds of nature around us. Birds. Water. The brush of air through the trees.

Then the roar of an engine. Fast. Powerful. Close. Logan's eyes go to the brow of the hill. His hand goes to his hip, he extracts his gun.

I turn to see what's got him so worried: a blacked-out van slowing down, the side door opening, someone with a gun leaping out.

Bullets hit the windshield of the Maserati. Logan and I run toward the SUV as he returns fire.

We lose them around ten minutes later once Logan heads onto the highway. We keep the silence going until we hit the city, parking up outside a townhouse in a quiet street.

"Let's go." The man is furious. His eyes bright with heat, his body tight.

We enter the house. It's devoid of any furniture.

"Upstairs, second floor, first room on the right."

"Where are we?" I look around. The house is cold. Utterly unwelcoming.

"Just get your ass upstairs."

I don't move. For one awful second, I think he's going to toss me over his shoulder. But instead, he takes a step toward me. Everything in my body screams for me to take a step back, but pride won't let me.

He reaches for my braid, which is peeking around my hip. He wraps it tight around his fist, pulling so that my head tilts back.

"Why are you so bent on putting yourself in harm's way?"

My scalp prickles, my eyes water. Not from his hold on me, but at the truth that is rising to my lips. It must blaze across my eyes like a banner, because he's got the measure of me.

"Cara, you've got to fight. Your mom fought."

I grow hot from the anger, the pain...the grief. "It didn't save her life."

He lets go of my hair. "You gotta try."

I slam my open palms against his chest. Bad idea, as the man doesn't move. He grabs me and before I know it, I'm over his shoulder, beating his back with my fists, screaming to be put on my feet.

I get tossed onto a bed, my hair exploding out of its braid, falling over my shoulders, my chest and lap.

"Perfect," Logan says.

I'm about to yell some more, when he goes for my hands. Quickly, he ties my hands together with my own hair. He reaches into a drawer beside the bed, pulls out a length of rope and binds my hair and hands to the ornate metal headboard.

"Very mature," I hiss, wriggling my hands, chest rising and falling, my feet digging into the linens. My hair fights the hold, but he's weaved the rope through the strands, trapping them as much as me.

"Stay." He grins, heading for the door.

"Fuck you, Logan!" I scream, as the door slams shut.

Long minutes pass with me trying and failing to get free. "Oh come on!" I pull, tug and hurt myself in the process, bruising my wrists.

I turn onto my left side, my arms twisting as I shuffle to my knees, "Yes!" I work the stiffness out of my fingers as I inch closer to the headboard. "Come on..." I loop a finger around a small lock of my hair and tug. It pulls free of the rope, creating some space. I groan as I begin the painful process of tugging more hair. Some of the strands break which causes me a physical pain in my stomach. I keep going, but soon it's too much. Too sore.

I wilt forward, placing my head on the metal, quietly sobbing. The few locks that are free rise up, patting my cheeks. I kiss them lightly and sit back on my heels, immediately feeling strong thighs either side of my hips.

Logan.

His hands come around my arms, moving down until he finds the knots.

"If I cut you loose, will you run?"

I shake my head, weeping. He edges closer, his chest against my spine. Heat blasts inward making me sit upright. His hands work quickly and the knife he's holding slices through the rope, avoiding any of my hair.

I massage my wrists once they are free, but my hair is whipping itself into a frenzy and tries to claw his eyes out.

"Easy..." He pushes the wayward locks down and back over my shoulder, "Don't make me tie you up again."

His words create a storm of sensation so new and so vibrant in my pelvis that I'm suddenly aware of the intimate nature of our positions.

His lips are at my neck, his breath a whisper across my skin. "Don't fight me." He takes one on my wrists. It's red. Bruises will form. "You're not used to taking orders are you, Princess?"

His voice is luscious and sexy. Slipping his hands under my shirt, he presses one across my lower belly while the other strokes my breasts, making me writhe. "You deserve passion, Princess. Not that vacant chaos."

Through the thin lace of my bra, he rubs both nipples, forcing me to search the ceiling with my gaze, my mouth open, my breath rough. "You deserve me, not those strangers..." One hand runs back down my torso to pop the button on my denims.

He slides his hand into my panties and finds what he's looking for.

"Logan!" I grind my hips, rising upward so that we both end up on our knees. The sob lifts in my throat as everything within turns electric. He rubs in a steady back-and-forth motion, before sliding the finger inside.

I lose it. Spectacularly. The orgasm is powerful and hurts like hell. I pitch forward onto the pillows, mumbling incoherently. He brings me down to the bed so that we are spooning, my hair looping around my head like a halo.

Logan finds my zipper, tugs my jeans down. I hear his fly, then his hips ease against mine, along with his erection. I moan again.

I feel him. Gentle and searching between my legs. I screw my eyes tight, muscles clenching. My hair is in a frenzy now, the locks undulating and reaching back for him.

He picks them up; I feel him turning his fist around the strands. "I'm going to have to tie you up again."

"Please..." My voice is steeped in passion, euphoria escaping with every breath. "Or my hair will keep trying to grab you..."

I feel Logan's laugh against my shoulder. He flips me onto my back. "Up."

I comply, curving my fingers around the metalwork again. My hair is desperately trying to reach for his...dear god...he's so big. He reaches for another piece of rope in the drawer and ties my hair around my wrists. Tight.

My jeans are pulled off and he shrugs out of his clothes. He's utterly nude.

"Ready?"

I nod eagerly. My hair might be trapped but it's singing, burning and digging into my skin.

He reaches into the drawer again. I expect more rope, but instead he pulls out a condom. I watch him roll it on himself, before running his hand down his length.

"Look up at me."

I lift my lashes. He reaches down and unbuttons my shirt, taking his time to kiss my torso until he reaches my bra. He grabs the knife, cuts it away, tossing it to the floor.

He puts his mouth on one nipple. Sucking. Hard. The strands go crazy and I get a sense of surging wetness below. His cock rests on my quivering belly. "Logan…" The woman saying his name like that has never existed before. When I was taken by others, I cried into my pillow or sobbed alone in the shower. But he wants me.

Not my hair.

He smiles. It's utterly sexy, masculine, and it makes me feel safe.

He finally lowers his lips to mine.

And I'm a changed woman.

I moan as our tongues touch, and I don't care what I sound like, or how I can't stop moving under him.

"Ready, Princess?" He reaches down, grasping his cock in hand before guiding the tip into me.

I arch into his chest. He's heavy and he doesn't shift, but I don't care. I want his weight, I want his body… I want his cock. I want it deep. I want him to take away all the terror.

And then he moves.

I lose it almost instantly, coming around him, blowing the dread right out of the water.

I've never, ever come like this.

Vacant chaos, Logan had called it.

But this…this is atmospheric, revelatory…

He's pressed so deep inside that when he retracts, it's breathtakingly beautiful. He crashes back inside of me, then withdraws, creating heat, comfort and a desire so deep that tears rush into my eyes.

"Here..." He makes me meet his gaze. It's dark, haunting. "I'm here."

I sob as another orgasm takes me.

He grabs my hips, the sensation in my hands long gone as my hair constricts hard. He fucks me powerfully, leaving me unable to form words. I sink into sensation, losing myself to whatever he's giving me.

Life.

Hope.

A reason to live.

I come again, and this time so does Logan, his hips pumping furiously before slowing down so that we lie body to body, sticky with sweat.

He pulls out and releases my hands. Taking them, he kisses my cold fingers, rubbing them back to life before reaching for the comforter and dragging it over the both of us.

I'm numb. Drifting. Unable to decipher space and time. But utterly aware of my hair, weaving itself around Logan's waist. Tight.

I wake to someone shaking my shoulders.

"Get up." Logan throws my clothes at me.

"What's going on?" I do as he asks, my hair whipping itself into a braid that I quickly tie with a band that I always wear around my wrist.

"Company."

Logan pushes me behind him as we travel along the upper hallway. A huge shadow leaks up the stairs, then clarifies as they hit the light of the upper hallway. It's the man from the hotel.

He comes at me with a knife in one hand and a gun in the

other. I see Logan raise his weapon…and then nothing. I swivel to face him…what the…? He's out cold on the floor. Jess stands over him; she drops whatever she was carrying. It thumps to the wooden floor.

"Jess?" I murmur, a chill running down my spine, "What…?"

Her smile twists. Her eyes are venomous. My heart caves in as she grabs me, displaying a strength I've never noticed. I am dragged screaming into my bedroom.

I scream for Logan, kicking, cursing, trying to bite and hit, but they manage to get me on my knees. Jess drags my hands behind my back.

This is what mom went through…

I suck in air choking on the betrayal. "Why…?"

"Not everyone is born with a silver spoon in their mouth," Jess hisses into my ear as the blade aims for my heart. "I got your mom…now it's your turn."

You gotta fight.

Expelling a war cry at that horrific revelation, I pull my wrists apart as hard as I can, making Jess lose her grip. I push, reaching for the man, his eyes, his face, anything that I can scratch. The knife nicks my arm and I cry out. He goes for my braid, but perceiving danger, the strands have knotted tightly at the base of my skull.

A shot rings out sharply. The man gives a sharp cry that ends just as quickly as it began. Another shot and Jess falls away from my sight line.

Logan keeps me upright as I sob in his arms. He takes me out of the room, while the authorities are streaming through the front door, the noise of activity deafening as people trail up the stairs.

"Are you okay?" His eyes blaze with pain. Blood is cascading down his neck, disappearing into his collar.

I nod shakily, trying to mask the hurt that's making my breath catch.

"Princess..." he says softly.

"I fought," I whisper.

He smiles, brilliant and unguarded. He palms my hair, the strands unlocking out of the braid, so that they can snake around our hips, pulling us together.

OUT OF THE WAVES

Rose de Fer

The ocean was a carpet of light, glittering beneath the sun. As the boat powered its way around the island the dolphins came out to play. They danced in the waves, their smooth bodies gleaming, their bright eyes shining as they leapt and splashed.

When the boat came to a stop a man stood staring out across the water, shielding his eyes from the sun. The dolphins frolicked below, calling to him in their language of clicks, squeals and chirps, demanding food. They were perfectly capable of catching their own fish but there was something special about being offered treats from the humans who seemed so fascinated by them. The man obliged by tossing fish to them, feeding them like pets.

In return the dolphins put on a show for him, lunging out of the water, flipping, spinning and diving back in again. They rose up on their powerful tails, churning the water and waving their flippers. The man smiled, enjoying their performance.

The dolphins enjoyed showing off and they had a strange

affinity for the man—in spite of everything. For there was something dark about him, and his gifts were not without a price. Occasionally he would lure them with treats, gaining their trust only to trick them. Ensnared in his net, they would thrash and fight but ultimately they were helpless as he towed them away. Where he took them no one knew, but the wild dolphins were able to convey messages back and forth and it seemed that the captured ones were unharmed. Some even enjoyed their captivity. They were well fed in exchange for doing what they did naturally—dancing and playing while groups of people watched and delighted in their antics.

Like the dolphins, Naiae was fascinated by the man. And she had loved him from first sight. He was beautiful in his alien way. Dark haired, lean and muscular. Sensual. There was a commanding air about him but his face, while stern, had something of kindness in it. Only the hardest of hearts could be unmoved by the dolphins' affection and he clearly loved them, no matter his mysterious actions.

Day after day, Naiae had found herself drawn to him, compelled to watch his interaction with her sea cousins. Something swelled inside her breast each time he reached down to stroke their sleek bodies, to feed them from his hand. What would he do if he saw her? What if she were to swim up to the boat and give him a display of her own? Sometimes late at night she would imagine herself caught in his net, her slender wrists entwined in its loops and knots, her tail bound. Helpless. Sometimes she even found herself wondering what it must be like to stand upright, to have legs and feet, to walk as humans did.

She wasn't supposed to be this close to a human, but she couldn't help it. There was a whole strange world above the water that she knew nothing about. How could she not be curious? More than that, how could the others not be just as curious? Her sisters were content to stay beneath the waves far out at sea, never coming to the surface at all.

One day Naiae had persuaded them to watch a fleet of fishing boats with her and they had gasped with horror at the sight of the men. Disgusted, they had dived back into the water, hurrying back to the deepest reaches of the coral reef where they lived. Naiae had watched them go, feeling confused and alone.

One thing puzzled her. Why had she not shown them the most appealing of the humans, her dark-haired man? Other people were merely a curiosity, but he was the most beautiful thing she had ever seen. Her sex pulsed with excitement whenever she thought of him and a hot flush came over her as she wondered whether a mermaid could couple with a human.

That was the day she had pulled herself up onto a rock and waited to see what would happen. The sun blazed down on her, drying her pale skin, her long golden hair and finally, her tail. She'd winced as the scales shrank in the heat and began to itch. The itching became a burning and grew from there to a piercing agony, as though her tail were being sliced by a sharp blade. She'd cried out in pain as a line appeared, running the length of her lower body. Her tail was splitting in two.

The pain was terrible, but there was something wildly erotic about it. It awakened unfamiliar sensations in her. Her body pounded with a fearful vibrancy and for the first time she could imagine how it might be to have long supple legs in place of a tail. She could feel the throbbing between them, in the place where her sex would be open and exposed, not concealed as it was with her kind. How would it feel to be touched there? To have a man plunge himself inside? To have legs to wrap around him as he did?

But the pain was building, becoming unbearable, and Naiae grew frightened. She'd only heard rumors of merfolk transforming, rumors involving pain and true love. But she couldn't remember if it was true love that could make her human or true love that could transform her back. No matter what, it couldn't be true love if only one heart felt it. She might be trapped in her legs forever, unable to see her sisters again or swim with her dolphin cousins.

Suddenly terrified and uncertain, Naiae had dived back into the water, where the pain gradually began to subside. She flicked her tail, relieved to find she hadn't injured herself too badly. Within minutes she was fully healed and she shuddered at the thought of what had nearly happened. If she had been able to endure the pain, she would have had legs. She would have been able to walk as the humans did. And possibly never have been able to return to the sea. The memory had haunted her ever since.

Every day she told herself that it would be the last time she would watch him, the last time she would drift in the gently rocking current, gazing at him and tormenting herself with thoughts of what might be.

And every day she found herself drawn back to the same spot, her heart bursting with love.

There was only one way to find out if he could ever feel the same about her. She would have to make contact.

She envied the dolphins their carefree existence, unhindered by rules about staying hidden. She was desperately curious about where he took them, what he did with them and why they didn't want to leave. They seemed frightened enough when they were caught. So that evening she followed him home.

The boat entered a lagoon and immediately Naiae heard the voices of her sea cousins. They were singing. She swam over to a mooring and her eyes widened at what she saw beyond it. A huge amphitheater curved around the edge of the lagoon. The water had been fenced off and dolphins splashed inside it.

This must be where people sat and watched. But watched what? Dolphins at play? Surely they only needed to stand at the edge of the shore to see that.

But as the dark-haired man left the boat and approached the enclosure she began to understand the special appeal. The dolphins met him at the edge of the stage, tossing their heads and splashing him, begging him to play with them. They had missed him.

He laughed and stroked them fondly, speaking to them in his deep resonant voice. Naiae could understand some of what he said and the words were filled with affection. The dolphins chattered back at him in their own language, although he could have no way of knowing what they said. They had a name for him: *U'hanei*. It meant "master."

Naiae trembled as she watched him instruct the dolphins. He stood on a tall platform and held a giant hoop out high over the water. A dolphin jumped up and soared gracefully through it to be rewarded with fish. A second dolphin repeated the maneuver and was rewarded as well. Naiae could almost hear the cheers of the crowd that must come to see these antics during the day. The dolphins performed trick after trick and Naiae wondered what it must be like to be taught to dance like that. To leap and spin in the air, to please one's master so and be stroked and praised and fed. She was determined to find out.

The next time he cast his net, he would be in for a surprise.

A few days later she was teaching herself how to jump and clear the water as the dolphins did. They watched her efforts with amusement before demonstrating how they did it. Naiae was so absorbed in learning what they were showing her that she almost didn't notice the boat when it came. Suddenly the wild dolphins were agitated. The man was setting up the net.

The dolphins splashed and chirped, sending warning calls out through the water. Naiae's heart swelled.

With barely a thought for what she was doing, she swam at once for the boat. She dived beneath it and waited. The dolphins followed her, nudging her and thumping her with their tails, nipping at her fins and urging her to escape. She smiled and stroked them, reassuring them that she knew what she was doing. Confused, they darted around the boat before finally leaving her to her peculiar decision.

The net plunged into the water, dragging behind as the boat began to move again. Naiae steeled herself and swam straight toward it. She thrust her arms through the holes and struggled to entangle herself further. The mesh pressed against her bare breasts, a tactile sensation both unfamiliar and thrilling. She knew from watching the man that her movements would alert him. Then he would haul the net up.

Sure enough, it began to close around her and she felt herself being pulled toward the surface. Her fear was almost as intense as her anticipation. How would he react when he saw what he had caught?

Naiae kept her eyes closed, listening to the gentle slosh of waves against the boat. She could hear the sound of the man's breathing as he reeled the net in. Then his breathing stopped.

When she opened her eyes he was staring down at her, a look of incredulity on his face. He'd been expecting a dolphin and now he was faced with something entirely other.

"My god," he whispered.

Naiae wriggled a little in the net, gazing up at him. Her hands were sufficiently tangled that she couldn't smooth away the wet hair from her face and even this small helplessness made her shudder with excitement. There was no chance of escape now. She was his, to do with whatever he wanted.

"Is this real?" he asked.

It's real, Naiae said, or tried to, but no voice came when she opened her mouth to speak. At least no voice he could understand. For she spoke only the language of the dolphins and to him her words would be meaningless sounds.

He stood staring at her for a long time, his gaze sharp and assessing. He was clearly pleased by her appearance. His eyes roamed over every inch of her and Naiae squirmed as she imagined his hands on her skin, her breasts, her tail. Perhaps one day even her legs. He crouched at the edge of the deck and reached down to touch her.

Naiae instinctively shrank back and the man smiled. He seemed to enjoy her timidity and she lowered her head submissively, savoring the moment. She closed her eyes as his fingers touched her face, exploring its contours. His hand was warm and the contact sent a surge of desire through her body.

When she looked at him again his smile had grown wider. And a little calculating. "I saw you the other night," he said, "only I didn't believe it was real. You're so beautiful."

She stared back, boldly meeting his eyes with a seductive smile of her own. Would he imprison her now, as he had the dolphins? Make her perform for treats like they did? She thought of being held captive and the image made her sex tingle. She flicked her tail, splashing him as she pretended to struggle.

He laughed softly. "Oh no, my sweet pet. You're not going anywhere."

Naiae floated in the fenced lagoon, wondering where the dolphins were. She could hear them so they must be somewhere nearby. Perhaps there was another enclosure next to the one she was held in.

He watched her closely as she swam back and forth, dived

down to the bottom of the pool, turned in circles underwater and splashed as the dolphins did. Each time she met his eyes she blushed and had to look away. U'hanei. Master.

He came to the edge of the pool and held out his hands. He beckoned her over and she swam shyly up to him, her tail flickering beneath her in the water. In his hands he held a clutch of bright red berries. She had tasted such things only once before, a delicacy someone had dropped into the sea. Blushing, she lowered her head to nibble the treats from his hand. Desire consumed her as he took her face in one hand and wiped away the juice from her lips with the other.

Then, smiling again, he turned and walked away. Naiae wanted to call out to him, wanted to beg him to come back, to swim with her, to plunge with her into the water and twine together as merfolk did when they joined. But he was heading for the strange square structure that must be his home. When he reached the door he looked back at her once. Then he disappeared inside.

Naiae's heart sank. So he didn't want her after all. So much for true love. With a lump in her throat she turned away and swam toward the far end of the enclosure. Was this how she was to spend the rest of her days, then? Tears filled her eyes and she dipped her head beneath the water. Down there she could pretend she wasn't crying.

She could see a wavering stripe of light rippling on the surface of the water. Curious, she peeked out and looked over at the house. He had left the door open.

Her breath caught in her throat. The light stretched toward her like a path and her heart began to pound. Was it a test? Had he meant for her to follow him? Could she?

She swam to the edge of the tank and hoisted herself out of the water. She rolled onto the dry grass and sat, waiting. Soon the strange burning pain began and she gritted her teeth, letting it wash over her. The tearing sensation wrenched a cry from her and she bit her lip, trying hard to keep silent. Her tail was separating, exposing her sex as her fins became flesh and the pain shaded into a kind of pleasure that was almost overwhelming. It was scary, exhilarating.

When at last the process ended she lay gasping and exhausted, her body aching from her exertions. She looked down at herself, at her legs. With tentative fingers she reached down to touch her feet, her knees, her thighs. The skin was so soft, the touch electric. She wanted to walk, to dance, but she wasn't even able to stand up. She simply didn't know how to use her legs. With a flush of desire she imagined her master teaching her, step by step.

She maneuvered herself up onto her knees and wriggled her toes beneath her bare bottom, delighting in the strange sensation. Again she caressed her thighs, relishing the feeling. She hardly dared explore further but her sex was yearning for contact and she could not resist. Gently she stroked the sleek wetness, sending a current of excitement through her that made her dizzy.

It was only then that she realized she was being watched.

Slowly she turned her head to see him. He was standing over her. Her master.

"Well, well," he said. He didn't seem surprised.

Naiae blushed and covered her face. A human woman might run, but Naiae wouldn't have even if she could. Her helplessness only intensified her desire and she wanted him more than she had ever wanted anything in her life. She murmured into her hands, secret desires and pleas he would not understand. But he didn't need language to know what she wanted.

He gathered her in his arms and lifted her up. Frightened and thrilled in equal measure, she didn't struggle. Instead she wrapped her arms around his neck and buried her face in his chest. She trembled as he carried her inside the house. They passed through two doors and then they were in what must be his bedchamber. He laid her down on a huge bed and she sighed at the tactile pleasure of the unfamiliar materials.

He watched her as she explored her surroundings, touching everything. The soft blankets, the airy pillows, the smooth polished wood of the bedstead. When she looked up at him again he was undressing. She gazed at his broad chest, his muscular arms and especially his legs. Her eyes stopped roaming when she saw his cock and she pressed her thighs tightly together, sighing at the jolt of pleasure that coursed through her.

Her heart began to pound as he approached her. She held still as he placed his hands gently on her feet. The exquisite touch made her cry out. She had never dreamt that skin could be so sensitive!

His fingers closed around her slender ankles and he firmly pulled her legs apart. Naiae didn't struggle or resist as he exposed the wet pink lips of her sex. The cool air caressed her, teasing her. She stared down at herself in amazement before looking back up at him.

He released her ankles and she instinctively closed her legs, uncertain what else to do with them. She regretted her reflex at once when she saw the slight frown on his face, but she couldn't find the courage to open herself again.

Her master shook his head and stepped away from the bed. Naiae thought he was disappointed. She wanted to call him back, wanted to say she was sorry. But he only went as far as the dresser, where he opened a drawer and took something out. She blushed to the roots of her hair when she saw the ropes.

"If you won't stay still," he said, his voice low. He didn't finish his sentence. He pushed her onto her stomach and brought the loop of rope down sharply across her bottom.

Naiae yelped, startled. Another stroke fell, this time higher up, on her back. Another landed across the backs of her thighs, then another across the tender soles of her feet. She cried out at each stroke. The rope stung terribly and made her writhe on the bed but it was also curiously arousing. Like the pain of her transformation, every stinging stroke only reminded her how wildly alive she was, how truly awake her senses were at last.

Again and again he whipped her, eliciting little cries and gasps from her. She clutched the pillow, letting the pain wash over and inside her. By the time he was through she couldn't tell whether it was pain or pleasure she was feeling.

Afterward he kissed her inflamed skin and told her she would have to learn to be more obedient. He eased her onto her back once more and she couldn't meet his eyes. Her face burned with shame and excitement.

She didn't resist as he wound the rope around one ankle and pulled it taut. Then he tied it to the end of the bed. Her punished skin burned beneath her and Naiae covered her face with her hands as he repeated the procedure with her other ankle. Her breathing grew shallow and she felt her legs forced apart again. Now she had no choice but to keep them spread.

But he wasn't content with securing her legs. He peeled her hands away from her face and tied her delicate wrists together, fastening them over her head. The position forced her back to arch, presenting her breasts for him. He cupped them, squeezing gently and tweaking the nipples into stiffness.

"Next time you disobey me," he said, "I'll whip you here."

Naiae gasped, both at the stimulation and the threat. Her nipples burned with the promise of such attention and for a moment she was tempted to resist him, to earn more punishment. She wanted to experience everything he could to do her.

But more than anything she wanted to make him proud of her, so she contented herself with pulling at the ropes to reinforce her sense of vulnerability.

Never had she dreamt that anything could be so exciting, that helpless submission could be such a heady adventure. Even without her bonds she was completely in his power, at the mercy of his calm authority.

"Now," he said, "let's have a good look at you."

A shudder ran the length of her spine as he stood over her, looking down at her splayed and naked body. He drew his fingers lightly over her breasts and down her breastbone, making her sigh. His fingers danced along her skin, awakening nerve endings she never knew she had. The soft hollow of her waist, the curve of her hip, the line of her thigh. All of it was a sensual experience beyond imagining. Her heart was racing, her blood pounding in her ears, deafening her.

Her legs were the most sensitive part of all, alive with tingling warmth. She whimpered softly as he squeezed her thighs, gently at first and then more firmly. At last his fingers slipped down into the delicate crease of her sex, where she wanted him most.

If she could have spoken his language she would have begged him to take her, to pin her down and have her, to make her fully human. If it meant forever, so be it. She tried to show him with her body that she was his and he seemed to understand. He lowered his head to hers and kissed her, pressing his lips to hers. Lust surged through her and she lifted her pelvis, offering it to him.

When he straddled her she couldn't help but stare at his powerful legs on either side of her, the muscles taut and sinewy. Magnificent. But his cock soon drew her attention. He angled himself against her dewy folds and she cried out as he entered her. Ecstasy spiraled through her as he slowly inserted himself inch by inch.

"There's a good girl," he murmured, pressing his full length into her, smiling as she gasped and tossed her head from side to side.

Good girl. She'd heard him say it to the dolphins. That meant he was pleased with her. She rocked against him and clenched the muscles of her sex, enjoying the answering pulse in his cock as he grew even harder inside her.

He fucked her then, filling her with long slow strokes, drawing out and waiting only to plunge himself back in again. Her legs burned with each thrust, a pleasure almost past bearing, and she wished she were free only so she might wrap them around his body. She might use her feet to drive him deeper, to help him pound her viciously.

Delirious with pleasure, she cried out, calling the name the dolphins had given him, calling him master. He fisted a hand in her hair as his pace quickened, and it wasn't long before she felt the first twinges of her mounting orgasm. It overtook her like a wave, drowning her in rapture as she screamed into the air, surrendering herself to the violent pulses as her body came alive in every possible way. Nothing beneath the sea had ever awakened such bliss in her.

She lay panting in the aftermath for several moments before he spoke again.

"My little pet."

Suddenly her eyes were blurring with tears and a lump swelled in her throat. She didn't understand her response. Her body was still vibrating from the excitement of everything he had done to her, the way he had made her feel. But suddenly she was gripped with a terrible sense of loss.

"Shh," he said, stroking her face. He didn't say anything else but she sensed that he understood her fear. Now that she was human, had she lost her magic? Would she become ordinary in his eyes now that he had tamed her?

"You're as beautiful as ever," he said, and she started a little at the idea that she had no secrets from him, that he could read her thoughts. "And I've always loved you."

He kissed her before the shock of what he had said could sink in. So all this time he had been watching her too. She could only gaze at him in wonder as he untied her and helped her to her feet. Her legs trembled but they held her and she felt another surge of longing as he led her outside. Moonlight rippled on the surface of the pool. When they reached the water's edge she hesitated, uncertain. So he pushed her in.

At once her legs began to burn and tingle with the now-familiar pleasure and pain. She flailed in the water and it took her several minutes before she realized what had happened. She was a mermaid again. Overjoyed, she performed a graceful dive, soaring high above the surface before plunging back into the water again. She swam back to her master and he leaned down to kiss her, cupping her face in his hands and smiling.

From somewhere close by she heard the dolphins calling her name, delighted that she was so near. And she closed her eyes and smiled as she imagined the wide-eyed faces of the crowd over the coming days as they watched the show, enchanted by the dolphins and the mermaid who danced in the waves at her master's command. Afterward she would perform again, out of the water, her legs trembling as he taught her a new way to dance.

YOUR WISH

L. C. Spoering

He stands at the window more nights than he does not. The land spreads out below him: hills and valleys, the meandering river. There are lights down there, an uneven spray decorating the landscape, marking houses, bars, the odd shop open this late, the police station. The house is built on the side of a mountain, like the Hollywood sign in old photos, like a crouching lion far above a sleeping city, and so he can stand there, back to the lavishly appointed living room, the state-of-the-art kitchen, the bedroom with a vast, low bed and expensive stereo system, all the trappings of the successful young bachelor.

He stands there, hands gathered behind his back, and I watch from my perch, tongue held fast by the proverbial cat, invisible but tenacious, and keep my own hands clasped in my lap so I do not fidget or fumble; I work my lip between my teeth instead, scratching an infernal itch.

"I think I'll go out tonight." This is the inevitable announcement and, every time, I exhale, trying to hide that combination of disappointment colored by elation that makes my chest contract painfully. I do hate when he leaves, even as I yearn for him to be happy, for once, forever.

"That would be nice," I say, and when he finally regards my reflection in the glass, I've worked up a smile with my abused lips, pink and swollen, but only from biting, only from the labor of my own teeth.

"I hope so." He heaves a sigh large enough, hard enough, that his shoulders go up and down a full several inches, and I can practically see the muscles strung taut and aching under his thin T-shirt, follow the contour with a fingertip I dare not raise. He never looks happy, even from the back.

When he turns, I consider the line of his jaw, the stubble that grows over it no matter how often he scrapes a razor along his face. He has something like movie-star looks, with soulful eyes and a faint smile, and I finally rise to my feet and pad noiselessly over to him to rest my hands on his shoulders.

He stands nearly a foot taller than I do, so my hands are almost held up above my head. That faint smile returns to his lips.

"You'll have a great time," I predict, though I have no idea: I don't go to these clubs he finds, the ones he drives down the mountain to, navigating the roads in a car that moves like a snake. He comes back from them smelling of cigarette smoke and spilled drinks, sweet and sharp, his pulse banging out the bass of the music, and I wonder why he goes back with hopeful expectations so often.

I also don't; I understand it in the same way I understand why one opens his eyes every morning, decides to face the day.

I let my fingers dig at the knotted muscles on either side of his neck and he relaxes under my touch. "You'll be okay here?" he asks, as he always does. It would be polite if it meant anything.

I nod, make myself smile, slide my fingers up along his neck, thumb tracing his jugular, but all motions as harmless as a kitten's. "Don't worry about me."

His smile is relieved and, for a moment, I wonder if he does wonder about my safety, my comfort, but then he pulls on his jacket, goes down to the car that purrs like a cat, like my touches, and I guess he does not.

Most nights he comes back, and stumbles toward the bed. I follow him, wait for him to waver, to stretch out on the bed, and then I undress him: shirt, pants, socks. I leave his underwear for last, carefully easing them down his thighs and off his feet. He visits the gym, but only grudgingly, and there is a slight curve to his stomach, the slope from his back to his ass, that would otherwise be obliterated by lifting weights or running for miles, without moving, on a treadmill.

These nights, his sweat stinks of beer, but I wipe his temples gently with a washcloth, and arrange him under his sheets and comforter, head nestled against his pillow. I wait until he is breathing evenly, and only then do I creep away.

Other nights, he brings a woman home. These nights, I stay out of sight, and he does not think of me. I'm allowed to watch: I don't know that we ever came to an agreement, as it is, but he's never asked me, never called me out, and so I watch, quiet, and try to guess what he sees in them, these creatures like painted nudes in a museum. I wonder.

He brings one home this night: blonde, long legs, a tattoo in the shape of a waning—or is it waxing?—moon above the cleft of her ass. She is beautiful, a face like porcelain and lips pink as cotton candy, both on her face and between her legs. He lays her out on the bed and presses her hands to the mattress with his, but I watch as she flexes her fingers and then pulls them away, wrapping her hands at his shoulders to push him, roll them both, over the rumpled comforter and dark sheets so she can climb atop him. She is majestic, a rider on her steed, hair tumbling over her back, but he looks shocked, and even as my cunt pulses just looking at her, I can't tear my eyes from him, from the look on his face, the way his expression only marginally changes when he comes.

She slips out before the morning light; he feigns sleep until she does. When she leaves, he sits up, scrubs his hands though his hair and calls my name.

I haven't made coffee, and I'm hardly dressed for attendance. Still, I stand, feet together, toes touching, in the doorway, waiting for him to speak.

"Well," he says, tongue thick and slow. "That didn't work."

I smile apologetically, touching my fingertips to my thighs. He sighs and looks down at the blankets over his legs, over the tips of his toes making mountains at the end, over the morning wood that tents the center.

"Can I help you?" My voice rises from somewhere in my chest and my cheeks flush, the heat evident even before the color, I know from experience. You'd think, after all this time, I'd have learned.

He shrugs, but he lies back again, almost reluctantly, and I feel my heart pulling in my chest as I walk the short distance around the end of the bed. The sheets are mussed so that they drape over the floor and snag under my knees when I lower myself to the rug.

"You don't have to," he sighs, folding his arms under his head.

"Yes, I do," I counter, but my voice is soft, and he accepts the blankets folded back, my hand around his cock, my mouth.

I'm told not to watch the next night, the next girl, but,

without something stuffed in my ears, I have no choice but to hear. I squirm in my spot, cross and uncross my legs, try to find some way to press against my aching clit that will render even the faintest relief. I feel bottled up, shaken, and wet enough to soak the cushion under my rump, streaks of my own juices discoloring the fabric from wiggling this way and that.

He walks her to the door in the morning; he makes his own coffee. I tiptoe into the kitchen, a kitten on light paws, holding my breath.

"I liked her," he notes, and though his back is to me, I can sense his smile. It makes my heart seize and pulse at once, and I nod.

"That's good," I say, touching my fingertips to my bare thighs; I rarely wear much, and it always felt natural, there in front of my master, to do as he pleased.

"That's what you've been looking for."

"Is it?" I open my mouth just to close it, and he turns to regard me, holding his coffee cup in his left hand. The sun streaming in through the window makes the hair there glint, like he might have a fine fur pelt under his bathrobe.

I shake my head. "I don't understand." I speak many languages, all of them, having been carted from one country to the next for years, for centuries: I've seen empires rise and fall, brave men turn to fools, the humble become wise.

"Maybe I've been doing it wrong." I can't decide if he's talking to me, or musing to himself, and so I stand still, measuring my breaths, the hair on the back of my neck stiff and sensitive.

"Maybe it's time to let you go." That is the feared answer, another thing I don't understand. I've been released before, over and over, but it's not in the way that is imagined. It's back in the bottle and off to the next, to bend to his will and serve, for many eternities.

I bite my lip and drag my gaze from his hands, wide and powerful. "And if I don't want to go?"

He looks surprised. He has dark, thick eyebrows, and they raise along his forehead, creating great furrows and deep lines between his eyes. "Why would you want to stay?"

That, I can answer, and I find myself smiling before I can stop the expression. "You." It's as simple as that, and his face grows more baffled, and, like it's a joke, he looks down at himself, as though the answer is in his sloppy morning dress, his bare feet, the slight paunch of his belly.

"Me," he says, looking up at me, doubtful. Surely he's thinking of the women he's brought home, the one from the night before who said please over and over until it stopped sounding like a real word.

I nod. "That's enough, isn't it?"

He doesn't reply, but his eyes go to the bottle on the mantle, long-necked and worn smooth, brass and shining silver, the handle seemingly delicate enough to snap. I follow his gaze, and we stand there for a long, silent moment.

"There's one wish left," he points out, and I shrug.

"That one's always the undoing," I say, gently. "Fairy tales get that one right."

He laughs, just a little, and I glow. He puts aside his coffee cup and crosses to the bottle, lifts it from the surface; the motion makes me feel seasick, and the taste of blood invades the back of my throat as he turns it in his hands.

"What if I make a wish for you, instead of me," he muses, and I shake my head. He expects that and gives me a heart-breaking smile.

"All right. What if I wish, for me, you."

I feel a tingle at the back of my neck, down my spine, along my sex. "Then that would be your command," I say, though, truly, I can never quite predict what might come of a wish. Like most, he wished for success first, and a company bore fruit around him. He wished for riches, and found himself waking in a vast apartment, driving down the canyon to his office in a luxury car. There was nothing unexpected, but, of course, isn't that when the guard is let down?

His thumb moves rings on the warm curved surface, and I press the crest of my thighs together in longing.

"Maybe I wish for you to stay forever."

I consider this and shrug delicately once more. "Then I'd have to stay." Would I be freed of my duties? Would the bottle shatter?

He sets it back down and my stomach clenches. "Or maybe I just never make that wish at all," he says, and holds out his hand.

"I could make you," I point out, but already I'm moving, already I'm smiling.

"You wouldn't," he predicts, and I shake my head, and my mouth opens easily under the warm pressure of his.

What is different about him that makes me cling to him now, fingers curling at his shoulders, toes clenching at the wool rug on the floor? I've been had by most of them, these men, but rarely have they had me. Truly, who can have an idea, a wish—who can possess a desire?

He does, he does, and the shackles he cannot see but I can feel, there around my wrists and ankles, they dissolve as he paces me back from the bottle, back from the room. I am feeling my way in expectation, heels lifted for the slick board that divides the doorway of his room from the hall, but he steers me, instead, past the long kitchen counter, out the open door.

The patio wraps around the house and, there, in the morning, the hills look parched and sparkling, as though the stars landed there for their daytime slumber. I can open my eyes and see the traffic stuck along the snaking roads, but he catches my chin before I can, thumb and forefinger, before his pinky rests at my windpipe. I'm held suspended in that position, and each breath pushes my throat against his finger, against that tiny pain, and I shiver, focusing my eyes on him.

"Say it," he commands, and my mouth parts again, the skin around my lips now burning from the roughness of his stubble.

"Say it," he repeats, and whatever sweet nothing might have been in his voice before is gone with the second demand; I feel weak, shaken, and my thighs slip against each other of their own accord.

"I'm yours," I say, without drawing my breath; it makes my chest hurt, a sort of dying exhalation—I wonder if that is what this might be, release from one world into another.

"Say it again." His hand moves from my chin, down my throat and over my bare chest. He parts the delicate buttons of my shift, and the fabric slides off me without protest.

"I'm yours." My head feels like, a balloon bobbing in the hot breeze. I can feel the same stir in the air at my ass and cunt, just before his hands, sliding over my hips and thighs to part my legs, spread my cheeks wide.

His finger toys with my asshole, and I let out a whimper.

"Again."

"I'm yours." My voice is high and strained, and I must lean against him in order to keep myself upright.

The patio railing leaves my feet dangling several feet off the ground once he has lifted me and deposited my ass there, and I sway with the breeze, with the sudden knowledge of the steep drop below me. The hill is decorated with boulders and razor-tipped cacti, a mile of hot sand, and I can feel it all at my back, even as his hold on me is steadying, comforting, safe.

"Again." The word brings my focus back to him, my gaze zeroing in on his mouth, before his eyes, as he loosens the tie on his bathrobe, dropping the garment, one arm at a time, on the boards below us.

"I'm yours." His cock is hard against my thigh, warm and solid, and I tremble; there is something new in this, though I am ancient and he is wise, and I feel the world tip on its axis.

He lifts me again, my legs around his waist, my fingers sliding into his hair. Every part of him feels more alive with each passing moment, lighting my nerves, making my head spin. "I'm yours," I offer, this time unprompted, but with a voice that is low and sure. "Forever."

His fingers dig into the skin of my shoulder blades as he enters me, hot and throbbing. I clutch at him as my cunt stretches and slips around him, the muscles rippling as though welcoming him home. My dizziness makes my mouth drop open, my moan audible on the hot air that swirls up over the rocks and back down to the valley.

He turns to face me over it, the sun that glints off the glass and chrome far down below, his cock pumping, sure, inside me. I'm already wavering there on the edge of an orgasm, toes curled on the crumbling precipice, when his tongue laps along my windpipe and jugular.

"Tell them who you belong to."

I'm whimpering, nearly unable to speak, but I am always his to command.

"I'm *yours*," I gasp out, and come.

THORN KING

Jane Gilbert

The forest is soft and quiet in the deepening evening.

I hurry along the worn track, instinctively increasing my pace as the leaves whisper to one another overhead, their smooth tongues chattering in the night air.

It's late. Much later than I anticipated being out, thanks to my spur-of-the-moment decision to wander off the regular trail. I'm tired, my feet hurt. All I want is to go home, sit on the sofa with a cup of warm tea.

The darkening woods scare me; when I was little, my mother used to tell me fairy stories—but not the soft, delicate ones. Oh, no. The creatures in her tales were frightening. Powerful. The fae, she used to say, have teeth as well as wings.

So intent am I on escaping the trees, the sultry shadows, that I don't see the froth of blackberry protruding across the path. Sharp strands catch at my calf as I hurry past and I cannot stop myself from yelping as the wicked thorns tear into soft, tender flesh.

I hobble to a nearby log and sit down to inspect the damage.

Blood. A lot. And I don't have anything with me to staunch the flow. Sighing, I stroke my fingers over the hot, moist stripe and prepare to stand, now more anxious than ever to be home. Only, when I look up, I find that I am no longer alone. Someone is standing in front of me.

It's almost impossible to make him out in the dim light—he blends so well with the forest around us—but I cannot fail to notice the citrine eyes glittering like fiery suns in his swarthy face.

He inhales deeply, and then, as if in slow motion, leans down to run a long, cool finger over the cut on my leg.

My heart almost stops in my chest and I barely manage to stop myself from crying out in fear as the tip of his digit skates across my skin and comes away wet with blood. He inspects it. Brings it to his lips, the smile he gives me as he tastes it almost feral.

Hungry.

He drops slowly to his knees, his dark head of hair brushing like seaweed against my bare leg.

Oh my god. Is he going to...bite?

The prickling fear crawling over my skin is almost unbearable but, far more disturbingly, I begin to feel a strange tingling low in my belly as the strands of his mane tickle my knee. It's like an electrical wire has short-circuited within me.

Just what is this...*thing*, this creature?

There is no time to consider the question; my mind blanks to a sheet of white nothing as a blisteringly hot tongue begins lapping at the crimson trails smearing my leg. I groan, my head falling backward like a heavy, dead weight. The feeling is...indescribable. Sublime. Completely foreign.

Arousing.

The idea that some strange being is tasting my blood—feeding on me—should fill me with horror. Yet, with each lick, blood rushes to my clit until it is so tight and swollen I feel as if it might burst. It's almost as if the cut in my leg has become a soft, luscious cunt and the tip of his tongue a tiny, rapacious cock.

I stare at the umbrella of leaves above and see a heavily pregnant moon shining between the trees. It leers down, a sinister voyeur to this strange, twisted encounter. His tongue continues to stab relentlessly. To probe at my flesh until it feels as if it has invaded my body, as if he's slid inside me like a dark, dark river.

I am drowning in him, beginning the climb toward orgasm, when firm hands tug me off the log and push me to my knees in the dirt. Somehow, I am naked—we both are—yet I don't remember our clothes being removed. I feel the damp earth against my shins, the rotting leaves sticking to my skin, the nagging, aching pulse between my legs. Those yellow eyes stare down, seeming to grow ever brighter as their owner looms over me: mesmerizing, frightening and awful and beautiful all at the same time. And they hold me in place like an iron band. Every thought I've ever had in my head has taken wing—flown far, far away—leaving only him.

He stands there like a conquering king, his body inches from my own, legs apart and his thick, angry penis protruding from the dark thicket between his thighs. A voice in a far-off corner of my brain tells me that he should be embarrassed by his nudity—that I should be embarrassed by my own. But all I can think about is how badly I want to touch him. How badly I want him to...devour me.

When he raises an arm, brings a hand to my jaw and grasps my chin with hard fingers, a little whimper, an unholy mixture of fear and delight, rushes from between my lips. His nostrils flare like a dragon's and he drinks in my response like a thirsty beast, sucking it deep inside his lungs. I close my eyes and lean my head in his hand, silently asking for something that I have no name for.

"Bleed for me," he growls, his voice curling through the dark forest like molasses, spreading like a deep purple stain in the night air. "Prove you are worthy."

It is command. It is a threat. It is the most terrifyingly arousing of challenges.

"Yes," I whisper, turning my head so that my lips touch the palm cupping my face. "Yes, my liege."

I don't know where the latter word comes from or why I say it; somehow, it just falls from my lips like a black pearl. Rolls like a marble into the black void between us. Delicate, precious, reverent.

His hand leaves me but I don't open my eyes straightaway, just let myself listen to the sounds of the forest around us. Feel his presence swirl deliciously at me. When I eventually lift my lids, I find him standing slightly farther away, but now he has a long, curling bramble stem in his hand, thick with thorns. His arm moves and the tip seethes across the dirt—hungry, looking for purchase—and, for a time, we simply stare at each other.

Beneath the weight of those yellow eyes, the cut in my leg begins to throb, my heart begins to ache and my skin begins to scream. I part my knees slightly, clasp my hands together behind my back and straighten my spine.

Blatantly offer myself.

He smiles, feral and fierce, and I watch, body taut with ravenous expectation, as the thorn whip leaves the ground and dances through the air. It hovers for a moment, flirting with the soft breeze—then comes down like a lightning strike over my bare breasts.

The barbs dig into the skin, calling forth drops of bright, red blood and I cry out from the pain. Cry out again as the bramble strand pulls backward and the hooky stem reluctantly relinquishes my skin.

It hurts. Oh, it hurts. I have never experienced anything like this; could never ever have imagined the intensity or how deeply I could feel the prick of a humble thorn.

Hot trickles chase one another over the swells of my breasts, spread out like tiny, red spiderwebs.

I am bleeding.

But then his tongue is there, that little sword of delight, probing each well of crimson, turning it into a bright pool of quicksilver, and I feel his calloused, clever fingers sliding between the moist, fluid-coated lips of my pussy.

"Beautiful." The word is hard, guttural—barely discernable, spoken as it is by the mouth pressed against my skin—and I feel like crying out with joy. I look down at the dark-haired creature pressed against me, watch his lips moving across my skin and feel my hunger, my craving for him, swell in my belly like a great, steep wave.

I want his tongue, his lips, on me forever but, too quickly, he raises himself, moves away from me, the thorny whip once again in his hand. I voice a protest, desperate not to lose him, but then those yellow eyes meet mine.

"Again."

It is harder to hold myself in position this time, knowing what is coming, but my desire to feel the prick of his lash is a hunger so consuming that I have no choice.

The bramble whip falls. This time without pause.

I moan and writhe as the barbed length pierces my skin over and over, feel myself growing wetter and wetter. It scratches relentlessly, the thorns like so many claws. How can the pain be so consuming? How can I want to push it away and welcome it at the same time? It is a puzzle, a riddle to which I have no answer. I am caught within a thicket so dense and deep that there is no way to untangle myself, no way out. More shockingly, as each lash falls, I find I have no wish to escape.

When the skin surrounding my nipples begins to weep red tears I suddenly find myself on my back, twigs digging into my skin, a pair of yellow eyes gazing down at me with adoration. Then they disappear from view and I feel like crying out in ecstasy as a tongue reverently licks at my abused flesh. But, this time, it is not enough.

"Please," I whisper brokenly. "Please."

I'm not entirely sure what it is I am begging for, but he knows. Oh, he does.

An arm snakes beneath me, rolls me over, jerks me roughly upward until I am on my hands and knees. I feel his wide, thick cock come to rest against the hot, swollen lips between my legs as he moves in behind me. Suck in a breath as one of his hands drops beneath us and gently explores the wet flesh just above his shaft.

I shudder, barely in control of myself. All I want to do is push against him, quench this raging thirst that has taken up residence in my body, but, sensing my intent, he removes his hand and instead plunges it into my hair, pulling me backward so that my hands leave the ground, and holds me in place.

His free hand brushes across my thigh, and I squirm slightly as I feel something sharp scratch the skin.

A thorn.

His hand leaves my hair, trails down my body to join its twin, and I go completely still. Feel my breath stall as his fingers delicately part my lower lips, exposing my clitoris.

"Say it," he rasps.

I don't pretend to misunderstand. His intent is crystal clear and I know exactly what the words—the ones flooding my head—will unleash if I let them loose.

I stand on the edge of the cliff, a bird about to take flight for the first time—and hurl myself over the edge.

"Yours, my liege," I breathe, bracing for the pain. "Yours."

The stab, when it comes, is twofold: a thick rod digging into the soft flesh of my cunt, the sharp prick of a thorn in my most tender knot of flesh.

I scream out like I never have.

The sensations are excruciating. Burning. White hot. I can't tell if I'm in agony or ecstasy. Can't feel my body anymore. Only him. And the brutal climax coursing through me. It stretches out, seemingly endless, until, finally, I black out.

When I open my eyes, it's morning. I'm in my own bed, tucked between soft flannel sheets. Pristine. White. Unstained by blood.

But there is a strange prickling sensation around my wedding finger. I examine my hand and notice a delicate circlet of brambles resting just below the second knuckle.

That night, when I take my walk, I make my way straight to the tangle of blackberry. Smile in delight at the yellow eyes flashing ravenously in the gloom. He is there, waiting for me.

I drop to my knees and await the pleasure-pain of his touch.

My liege. My master. My Thorn King.

THE WITCH'S SERVANT

Michael M. Jones

Emmaline, once a princess and now a common servant, knelt before her mistress, the infamous Witch of the North Woods, waiting with infinite patience for the other woman to speak. Though her muscles trembled and her legs ached from holding absolutely still for what seemed to be hours, she neither twitched nor complained. Complaints earned punishments, and the Witch was so very, very good at delivering punishments. Even thinking about the Witch's deft hand with a switch across her breasts or bottom was enough for Emma to shiver—with anticipation and never-voiced desire, not fear. She could feel the trickle of moisture between her legs. She dared not squirm to address the itch. She remained still, hands folded on her thighs, gaze cast downward to the rough wooden floor.

"Seven months," stated the Witch, voice low and smoky, dark eyes fixed unwaveringly on Emma. "That's how long you've been with me, girl. Seven months since you came to my door, all full of fire and arrogance, a spoiled brat of a princess demanding food and shelter."

Emma did not speak. She had no permission. She acknowledged this with a dip of the head, long ebony hair rippling with the movement. The Witch loved her hair. Loved to yank it hard to get her attention. Loved it when Emma wove it into a tight braid, all the better for tugging.

"Seven months since you slept in my bed without asking permission, assuming that as a princess you deserved the best accommodations in the house. So used to having all you desired, you never even saved me a share of my own dinner. You laughed when I asked you to fetch firewood, openly mocked me when I suggested you get water from the stream, refused to lift a hand."

Emma flushed with shame, pale skin turning beet red with embarrassment. She'd been so full of herself, so haughty, that day. So blind. She'd seen a peasant woman living alone in the woods, half a day's walk from the nearest village, and never even once thought *witch* or *trap*. She'd been lost, cold, hungry, tired, frightened, and she'd repaid her hostess with...well, with unthinking contempt. She'd deserved everything she'd gotten as a result.

Well, not everything. That week she'd spent coughing up toads and snakes had been the most miserable, nightmare-inducing period of her life. After that, she'd accepted the more physical punishments, even come to welcome them as a sign of the Witch's growing forgiveness.

"Seven months since a princess walked through my door," murmured the Witch. From where she sat, in the cottage's one truly comfortable chair, she could just reach out and touch Emma. She lifted one bare foot, bringing it up under Emma's chin, forcing the younger woman to finally look up and meet her gaze. "In that time, I've turned a disobedient child into a capable servant. One might even call you competent…acceptable if her standards weren't too high."

Emma bit her lip to keep from stammering out words of thanks. The Witch was notoriously stingy with her praise. From experience, Emma knew that "acceptable" was exceptional anywhere else. Her nipples tightened with a rush of emotion. She'd pleased the Witch. So why did something feel different about this conversation? She regarded her mistress, drinking in the sight with a rare boldness. When she'd first arrived, she'd taken the Witch for an old hag, decrepit and harmless. When the Witch had raised her power and laid down the first of her curses in retribution, Emma's impression had shifted to one born of fear, resentment and anger. But now…now she saw the beauty, unconventional though it was, in those stern features and flashing dark eyes, in the long dark hair streaked with silver, in the sturdy body and generous curves. The longer she'd remained with her mistress, the more Emma had come to separate truth from illusion, style from substance. The Witch was older than her, yes, but hardly an ancient crone. More like a woman in her prime who had no need or desire to attract suitors, who held off the world with an utter lack of caring. The Witch was, Emma thought, quite lovely indeed. She wouldn't mind being that comfortable in her own skin when she was that age. Not like her mother the Queen of Rosedale, whose beauty was artificial, fragile and expensively maintained.

"Your time with me is at an end."

"What?" gasped Emma, forgetting all the rules in her surprise.

The Witch's hand was quick to lash out, her palm leaving a bright stinging mark on Emma's cheek in its wake. "I did not give you permission to speak!"

Emma gulped, nodding without looking away. Her eyes watered, more with surprise than with pain. It was impossible to separate the threads of her emotions: the very brief resentment at being struck and the relief that her mistress cared enough to remind her of her place.

"As I said, your time with me has come to an end. You came here as a princess, became a servant, and are free to leave as whatever you want." The Witch did not smile, but something in her tone softened. "There are rules to this, things which I may and may not do. I may curse you for being a bad guest. I may not turn you into a statue and leave you outside for the birds. I may keep you until I'm sure you've learned your lesson. I may not force you to stay longer than that. That would be wicked. And we all know what happens to wicked witches."

There were always heroes available to slay the ogres, dragons, and witches who stepped outside the boundaries. That was simply how things worked. Emma's father had earned his bride and his kingdom that way, once upon a time.

"The point is," said the Witch, "that while I have found your services to be...occasionally satisfactory, I must set you free. And as is proper, I wish to offer you a gift." There was a long, awkward pause, the Witch watching Emma expectantly, Emma's mouth suddenly bone dry, heart pounding. Free? She was a free woman again? After her time here, she wasn't even sure what that meant. The Witch huffed impatiently. "I grant you permission to speak your mind, girl. In fact, I grant you permission to do whatever you desire. I am no longer your mistress."

Emma tried to read the Witch's tone. It held the same sort of fond exasperation it always did when she was slow to interpret orders, or pick up on a new skill. Was the Witch happy to be rid of her? Would she miss Emma like one might miss a family pet or favorite cow? "A gift?" she asked, forcing the words past the desert of her lips and tongue. She did not move, not even sure her muscles would obey her if she tried to stand. Her thighs, bare under the short shift she currently wore, were bone white where she'd unconsciously pressed against them.

"A gift. Shall I enchant you to speak rubies and cry pearls? Do you desire unspeakable beauty or the language of the birds? All these and more are within my scope. I could give you a tablecloth that conjures feasts, a drum that summons armies, a tinderbox that commands demonic dogs. I can arrange love at first sight with the prince of your choosing, or bless you with perfect children." The Witch held her hands out, summoning phantasmal images and fleeting glimpses of untold riches and impossible wonders. Emma regarded the strong hands and capable fingers, and imagined them being used for more earthy pleasures. Her cheek tingled where she'd been struck. Her thighs were both hot and cool with inexplicable arousal. She drew in a slow breath.

"None of those," she whispered. "I want none of those, mistress."

"I am no longer your mistress," said the Witch, the simple statement cracking Emma's heart in half. "And what do you want if not beauty or riches, love or magic? Do you wish to be a queen? For that is possible. I could send you home on a flying cloud or in a carriage pulled by snow-white steeds." Her eyes glittered, stars deep in their depths. "I can give you the world, girl. Name your price." Was there something challenging in her words? Was this a test?

Emma swallowed, hard. "I want..."

"Yes?" The Witch drew forward, impatience coloring her words.

"I want...mistress, may I speak frankly? Truly so?"

"Yes, yes!" Emma knew that dangerous tone well. She was

pushing the Witch's limits. Sometimes she tested those boundaries on purpose. But this would be a bad time. Possibly.

Emma reached deep for courage, finding a tiny trace of Princess Emmaline of Rosedale, wearing her like a coat, knowing she needed some of that reckless confidence once again. "I want *this*, mistress." She used the word like a title, granting it power and meaning. "I don't want to leave. I don't want to be a princess, or a queen, or a free woman. I don't want to be a merchant's wife or a questing heroine. I want to be...yours." The depths of longing that poured from her lips shocked her, but the dam, once burst, could not hold back the torrent any longer.

The Witch cocked an eyebrow. Steepling her fingers, she regarded Emma solemnly. "Go on," she said, voice entirely neutral, neither accepting nor condemning.

"Mistress," Emma continued, "when my parents sent me on this quest to prove myself, we all knew what would likely happen. A horrible fate would befall me and I'd never come home, or I'd meet my future husband and become someone else's problem. Either I'd never be seen again, or I'd win my fortune and become useful. Usually, there's very little need for an extra daughter, except to secure an alliance." She heard the bitterness and knew that this was what she'd never wanted to admit out loud. "My older sister Angelica, she'll be married off for politics or as a reward to a giant-slayer. My little sister Juliana, she'll turn out to be the heroine of her own tale and win love for love's sake. The middle daughter's tale never ends happily. Here, with you...this is where I belong. Not as a princess."

"I see," murmured the Witch. Her hand crept out to caress the same cheek it had slapped not so long ago. Emma leaned into the cool touch, eyes closing of their own accord. She nuzzled the touch, an unspoken craving satisfied. The Witch could be stern yet fair, harsh yet understanding. "You would rather live as a servant to a Witch, than return to an unhappy life of riches."

"Yes, mistress," whispered Emma. "I look back at who I was, and I hate it. You taught me discipline and the value of hard work. You made me better."

The hand left her cheek, long fingers instead running through Emma's hair, untangling the silky strands. Though the Witch had worked her hard day and night, forced her to fetch and carry, cook and clean, she'd always insisted that Emma keep herself clean and well groomed. "I refuse to be served by some filthy ash-grubber," she'd snapped repeatedly. Indeed, a lack of cleanliness had warranted punishments...and Emma occasionally "forgot" a stain or smudge because of it. The Witch had a deft hand at scrubbing her to within an inch of her life when that happened. Emma inwardly smiled at the memories stirred by the thought. "Please, mistress," Emma pleaded, "let me stay here to serve you."

The Witch's fingers tightened in Emma's hair, clenching a fistful of ebony locks, holding Emma's head still while she studied the princess's eyes. "Not a drop of deceit or falsehood in you," the Witch said in approval.

Emma wondered how well the Witch read her. Did she detect the catch in Emma's breath, the shiver that went right to the core where her pussy ached with fresh arousal? She was giving herself to the Witch...and it had a maddening effect. Not a drop of falsehood, true, but she was wet nonetheless. She licked her lips. "I mean it, mistress."

Evidently, the Witch was satisfied with this. She released Emma, leaning back in her oversized chair. "I understand, Girl." And when she said it, Emma knew that something had changed. A fundamental shift in the dynamic. Before today, she had always been "girl," the casual description of the Witch's servant, because names had power and the Witch played with power. But now...she had been Princess Emmaline. She'd become Emma. She was Girl. With her hands still folded neatly in her lap, she squirmed ever so slightly, trying to relieve some of the building tension, desperately yearning to touch herself, the need like an unreachable itch.

"I didn't say you could move, Girl." The Witch's tone was sudden and sharp; Emma froze under its weight. "I definitely didn't say you could pleasure yourself."

Emma turned a furious shade of red, pleased and embarrassed to have been caught, called out like this. "I apologize, mistress."

"I understand everything. You don't wish to stay here because you enjoy hard work. You don't like cooking and cleaning, and you don't want to be a drudge. You want to stay because you're still a spoiled, self-indulgent, hedonistic brat, a princess who thinks only of her own desires. Isn't that so?"

"N-no, mistress. I mean, yes, mistress."

"Admit it!"

"It's true, mistress," murmured Emma, hanging her head so she couldn't meet those stern, calculating eyes any longer. "I am a spoiled, self-indulgent princess, and I must stay with you until I've properly learned my lesson."

"Something tells me it could take a very long time. You strike me as stubborn and willful."

"I am, mistress." Emma struggled to keep the smile from her lips, forcing herself to maintain a stoic, even shamed, manner.

The Witch stood, then, for the first time. She closed the distance between them with a step. Silently, she gestured for Emma to rise. Emma did so, on shaky legs that threatened to buckle at first. Only several deep breaths allowed her to stay upright, and she was painfully aware of the arousal that slickened her thighs. A wayward gasp of pleasure and pain slipped free, disguised as a breath.

The Witch's fingers danced in the air like an artist at a painting, and the rough fabric of Emma's gray shift obeyed, seams parting and threads unraveling. The garment practically dissolved in the wake of the Witch's power, reweaving itself into thin, long strips. Emma was left naked, shivering in the unexpectedly chilly air, bare skin flushed with arousal. With her slim curves, boyish hips and small breasts exposed, she experienced an acute vulnerability. The Witch had seen her naked many times before, but this...this was different. Her nipples drew painfully tight with the rush of emotion. She licked her lips, trying to restore some moisture to them.

The Witch continued to work with a storm cloud's intensity. As Emma remained still, the strips of fabric danced and spun in the air, diving at Emma like an owl after a mouse. Suddenly, a pair of strips spun forward to wrap around her wrists. They tugged her hands behind her back, weaving together in a complicated, though not unbearably uncomfortable manner. Her arms secured behind her, Emma was forced to arch forward, breasts thrust outward like an offering. The Witch's smile was wicked with approval. She tapped Emma on the shoulder, forcing her to kneel once more.

Awkwardly, Emma sunk to her knees, maintaining her balance only through memory of the dance lessons she'd had once upon a time. More strips of fabric swooped down to secure her, tying together her ankles, winding around her legs and thighs, arms and stomach, looping between her legs and tugging upward. She gasped again, this time audibly, as she felt the pressure against her pussy, the fabric nestling between her lips where it teased her already aroused sex. If she wriggled ever so slightly, the cloth caught her clit in just the right—

"Stop that!" The Witch flicked a finger, and an errant strip echoed the movement, striking Emma's nipple. Surprised, she moaned, but froze. "You do not have permission to pleasure yourself, Girl. You will not orgasm until I say so."

"Y-y-yes, mistress," whimpered the increasingly frustrated Emma. Satisfaction was so close, yet so far away. That was enough to send another shiver through her aching body.

The Witch stepped back to admire the artfully trussed Emma, whose range of motion was dramatically limited due to the criss-crossing strips of fabric, which left so much of her exposed. She dipped her head in satisfaction. "You look quite nice like this, Girl. This bodes well for your future with me." She ran her own fingers down the front of her dress, and the fabric peeled away neatly, pooling around her feet in a rustle of fabric. Unapologetically, gloriously naked, she stood before Emma. There was no question that even without clothes, she held all the power. "You will pleasure me to the utmost of your abilities. Failure is not an option. I will tell you a story as you do so, and this may determine...our relationship moving forward."

Emma's eyes widened as she watched her mistress, nodding as best she could in acknowledgment. The Witch stepped forward again, her own sex mere inches from Emma's face. "Oh yes," murmured the Witch. "One more thing. If, at any time, this proves too much for you, if you cannot take it any longer and wish release, you have but to speak a single word." She bent down, and whispered the word into Emma's ear, breath hot against sensitive skin. "Rapunzel." The word echoed and rang within Emma's head, taking root with undeniable permanence. That word promised trust and security, safety and escape. Emma silently vowed never to use it unless the circumstances were dire indeed.

The Witch stood, and rested her strong hands on Emma's

shoulders. Emma understood her duty; she dipped her head forward to nuzzle between the Witch's legs, eagerly seeking out the surprisingly damp pussy with lips and tongue—the only parts of her she had free to use. The Witch smelled dark and musky, like the depths of the woods and strange herbs and a woman in her prime; it intoxicated Emma, and she drew in the scent with wild abandon. Her tongue flicked out to taste the Witch, and the outside world all but vanished.

"I was just like you, once upon a time," murmured the Witch. There was a catch in her voice as Emma licked her, a tightening of the fingers. "An extra daughter. Unwanted, unneeded, a political tool without a future of her own." Another pause as she shifted ever so slightly to allow Emma's tongue greater freedom within her. "I was willful, like you. Unwilling to accept my fate. Moreover, I knew I would never bow to any man and allow him power over me. I left home, and never looked back. I sought out hidden powers and had my share of adventures before I finally settled into my life as the Witch of the North Woods."

The words flowed over Emma as she dedicated herself to the task—no, the joy of pleasuring her mistress, of lapping and teasing at the soaked pussy, of licking and sucking the bud of her clit. It was hypnotic, almost transcendent, with every twitch of the Witch's fingers or hitch in her breath telling Emma that she was doing it right. Her own sex ached, throbbed against the fabric stretched between her lips, begged for satisfaction and release. She would have screamed with frustration were she not so pleasantly occupied.

"When you came along, Girl, I saw a kindred spirit. Oh, I could have cursed you with toad-speech and sent you on your way. Or covered you in tar and feathers, or any one of a thousand fitting punishments. But I knew that, given time, you had potential." The Witch's smile was a cross between smug and anticipatory. She removed one of her hands from Emma's shoulder to caress her own plump breast, tweaking a nipple with a moan. Emma felt it, somehow, the sensation reverberating through them both; she stilled briefly and the Witch's fingernails dug into her shoulder sharply. She redoubled her efforts. "I took advantage of the rules to keep you for the full length of time, exchanging the greater curses for the opportunity to help you find what you were made of. Thus far, I am not disappointed."

Emma tightened and released her thighs, trying to find some sort of relief from the constant pressure. She dared not admit it, for fear of her mistress's displeasure, but her tongue was getting tired. Every part of her ached—her legs from maintaining the position for so long, her breasts from the way she was bound, her pussy from the arousal. Pain, pleasure and need wove through her in a delicious tapestry of sensations, topped off with the heady taste and smell of the Witch. She felt the words more than heard them, embracing their meaning without dwelling over it. She understood what her mistress was saying, where she'd come from long ago. They were two of a kind. She was home at last.

The Witch must have sensed that her servant girl was starting to flag; she suddenly pushed Emma away. Before Emma could do more than whimper, the Witch snapped her fingers. The cloth strips binding her loosened, falling to the floor all around her. Her pale skin was marked with stark white strips that swiftly reddened. Emma nearly swooned with a new palette of sensations. The Witch sank back into her chair, legs spread, hands roaming her body in a lush, sensual manner. "Finish the job," she commanded, "with your hands if need be."

Though her body still tingled with pins and needles where full circulation had yet to return, Emma didn't even hesitate, diving between the Witch's legs with a desperate need to please, to see this through. She slid several fingers into the Witch's slick pussy, thrusting deep and quick, feeling the muscles clench, hot and tight, around her. Emma had never been with a woman before—never even known that it was what she wanted until now—but it felt natural to do this, right and perfect to lose herself in her mistress's depths, fucking her with fingers that alternately plunged and curled, moving with raw instinct.

It didn't take long at all; soon, the Witch captured her questing hand deep within, held it tight while her entire body rocked and shuddered. Low, guttural moans of ecstasy rolled forth from parted lips, fingers flailing before finding tight purchase in Emma's hair, tugging almost painfully. Wave after wave of orgasm swept through her, and Emma dove back in to desperately lap up the Witch's juices, drinking deep of their shared pleasure. She almost forgot her own unfulfilled need, until her body reminded her with a single insistent pulse. She groaned against the Witch's sex, pulling away only when the Witch tugged her free. "Enough, Girl!" she commanded, voice ragged and hoarse. "Enough."

Emma slowly regained a measure of her senses. The Witch's scent still clung to her, intoxicating and arousing, and she drew it in with a long breath. She'd done her duty, satisfied her mistress. She could be happy with that. Her own desires...they could wait, she supposed.

But the Witch had other ideas. She reached out, took Emma in her arms, drew her in for a long, hot, sensuous kiss. Lips parted eagerly, tongues danced and the Witch tasted herself on Emma. Something crackled and sparked between them, and magic poured through their joined bodies, swirling under the skin and deep into their cores. Emma, caught up in the kiss, lost in the unexpected intimacy and delight, was thus surprised when the Witch suddenly slid several fingers into her sopping pussy. "Come for me, Girl," she commanded at long last.

The hours—months?—of pent-up frustration and torment, combined with the sheer unexpectedness of the Witch's actions and her granted permission, was enough to send Emma into a screaming orgasm, her entire body convulsing as her senses exploded. Long moments passed before she came back to herself, crying with relief and joy and a dozen other emotions.

The Witch held her, more gently than Emma ever could have expected, stroking her hair, whispering soft reassurances, her very tone promising love and protection. Emma accepted this, too wrung-out to object. She merely curled up against her mistress, her lover, basking in the contentment.

Eventually, they moved into the bedroom, where Emma curled up against the Witch in the soft bed she'd only slept in once before, back when she was a spoiled princess. "Tomorrow," stated the Witch, "we shall discuss the new rules at length. For what we are embarking upon...is as complex as it is rewarding. But for now, sleep, Girl. Sleep, Emma."

But Emma was already drifting off, oblivious to the Witch's use of her real name. And when the Witch softly whispered her own true name into Emma's ear, the former princess merely smiled, lost in her dreams.

In the days to come, word would spread of the Witch of the North Woods and her new servant, the young woman with the mild manner and the playful eyes, who seemed content with her lot in life and who, if so inclined, might give a wandering prince or questing heroine a word of advice on how to best approach her fearsome mistress. And if such subtle disobedience earned her a punishment...all the better.

They definitely lived happily ever after.

MINE UNTIL DAWN

Valerie Alexander

The winter moon brooded over a deserted, driftwood-strewn beach. Perhaps it was my imagination but I thought I could feel a pining echo of loneliness ringing over the sand, like the reverberation of a heartsick bell that, rung once, echoes forever. It was hard to say if it was my own loneliness I felt so keenly on this night, or that of my ocean sisters. Centuries ago the locals drowned witches off these shores; ever since my family has communicated with their watery spirits, through spells honed and passed down through the generations. But now I was the only witch left of my lineage, and my moonlit beach rites left me lonely.

You wouldn't be lonely if you were with him, whispered the wind. I ignored it. My hopeless, one-sided love tortured me enough, whether I was cleaning offices at work or dealing out tarot cards at home. Tonight I couldn't afford to sink into despair. Tonight was to be a night of power—the night I won my love through witchcraft. Though only temporarily.

Justin's green eyes and deep voice rose up in my mind, his commanding panther-like walk and his luxurious coal-black hair. That careless, devastating smile that undid me whenever I saw it. But I shook it all away and began my spell.

I kneeled in my black nylon slip over the smoking charcoal, sprinkling the herbs of deer-tongue and witchgrass on the glowing embers. No one would bother me here tonight. They were all at the Winter Ball. Which was where I would be soon enough—after I cast a spell for the crime of my ugliness to be lifted, a spell to be beautiful for one night, to taste the power of bringing Justin to his knees, begging for me as I ran my hands over his muscles. His cock mine to command.

I'll never tell which spell I used. It was my formula, born out of much research pouring over old grimoires and my former sorcery experiments with my lost sisters of the sea. They were always there for me in every beach rite, bringing me an ocean gift for each spell that would do my bidding. Those gifts hung around my neck now: a string of perfect black pearls, glowing with violet and peacock-green shimmer in the candlelight. And as I chanted my incantations now, the waves crashing higher and washing up on the sand, I could see the faces of my ancestral witches in the surf. And then one wave roared even higher on the sand, almost to my feet...and receded to leave glimmering in the moonlight, another perfect black pearl.

I added it to my string and looped them over my neck. Immediately I began to change. My skin, my hair, my breasts, my waist, my feet. I began to chant a new incantation, swaying under the moon. I was an animal, a goddess, a sorceress. The cool tingling of the pearls sent a rush through my blood. And then I fell on the sand, so dizzy the night went black...and then I stood up.

I was beautiful now. I pulled down a long strand of my former mouse-brown hair; it was now a rich and glossy chestnut, my skin smooth and golden. My black nylon slip was an iridescent green gown now—a clingy silk that cupped my fuller, rounder breasts and narrow waist. Eagerly I pulled up the dress to view my long, well-shaped legs and high heels.

Yes, Justin would never resist me now. My night of love was here at last. I blew a kiss of thanks to my ocean sisters for lending me this predatory allure. Then I extinguished the candles and headed into town. I knew exactly where I was going.

The Winter Ball was being held at the grandest hotel in town—owned by Justin's family, of course. His family owned almost everything in town; they owned property, they owned stores, and they owned the company where I worked. All of my coworkers would be there tonight—the sleek executives and beautiful ambitious women who were too superior to talk to me—Cynthia, the cleaning girl. Of course their families had always feared my family, as we were well known in town as witches. Or rather, we had been once. When my mother died too young, there was no one to take care of me—and Justin's father's company had agreed to help me by giving me a job cleaning their offices. Only a tender sixteen, I had wanted to finish school. But I had to eat and finally I'd accepted the job.

I'd been there four years now, watching those manicured women striding through the corridors, tanned legs flashing under short skirts, greeting each other with bright empty smiles. Most of them had tried unsuccessfully to capture Justin; few bothered speaking to me, the lowly cleaning girl, who emptied their trash cans and wiped down their desks. Some were nervous—the older ones, who knew of my family's reputation for witchcraft.

And then there were the spiteful ones, who enjoyed mocking me and sometimes said, *Did you ride your broom to work,*

Cynthia? Hey, Cynthia, can you cast a spell for the winning lottery numbers? Oh wait, if you could do that, you probably wouldn't be a janitor. They'd laugh and laugh. Silly, dumb, Cynthia. I never said a word, for I needed the job and it's too easy to claim missing money and blame it on the cleaning girl. Other than throwing a few minor hexes their way, I stayed stoic. And truth be told, I couldn't bear the thought of leaving my job, if only because it meant I would no longer see Justin every day—the arrogant, handsome scion of the business, whom I despised even as I longed for his hard beauty.

At last I reached the hotel. As I walked up the steps, a murmur swelled amongst the photographers covering the event for the local paper. "Miss, your name? Miss!"

No one knew who I was. They only knew I was beautiful. The admiration felt like a symphony ringing in my ears.

Inside an orchestra was playing. Yet there was a pause in the chatter of the crowd as everyone looked at me with curiosity—the women with competition, the men with heat and hunger.

I gave them a gracious smile, as if I were born to entering ballrooms. I walked forward in my new spike heels, my gown swishing around my shapely legs, and felt my pearls humming on my neck. Then I saw her in a mirror mounted on the wall: a stunning young goddess with an angelic face and the voluptuous body of a silver screen movie star.

It was me.

I walked forward, aware of the men pleading with their eyes. *Me. Choose me.* But I wanted the prize, the prettiest and most confident man in the room.

My heart began to pound with some supernatural knowledge. I turned to meet Justin's green eyes.

"Please," was all he said, one hand extended in invitation.

We danced. There was a waltz, violins and moonlight on the

piazza. *Don't think this is romance, Cynthia. This is predation, carnal and sweet. Protect your heart.*

"You're so beautiful."

I traced his upper lip. So many times I'd gazed at his perfect lips when he worked late at night. "Not as beautiful as you."

There was so much I wanted to ask him. *When you smiled at me last month, you looked almost tender. I caught you watching me when I was wiping off your father's desk. Yet so many times you've ignored me. Could you love the girl I really am? Or only this imposter in your arms?*

Instead we waltzed, my eyes never leaving his. My spells were spells upon spells, like a mansion of interlocking rooms.

I looked at the great clock in the ballroom. Almost midnight. Sunrise was only a few hours away; it was time to act now, if I wanted to take the time to savor him.

I leaned my head against his chest. "There's so much I want to do to you..."

"Anything." His voice was hoarse, almost pained.

I scratched one fingernail lightly over his lip. "Then I must be alone with you now."

The three stories of his mansion loomed in the moonlight. He soared around the circular drive with careless perfection. He was impatient to be inside with me.

Out into the night air. I could smell a stable, not far off. Inside the carved oak door, he pushed me against the wall and kissed me. His mouth was hard; his teeth grazed my lip. I pushed him away.

He pulled me against him and kissed me just as brutally. "Enough teasing."

I pushed him back again. "I'm in charge here."

We stared at each other in the hazy moonlight filtering in the bay windows. His green eyes were burning, hungry, but uncertain of just what kind of woman I was.

Then he smiled his devastating smile. "Okay."

His bedroom was more spacious than my cottage. I retained a cool face as he reached impatiently to take off my dress.

"No," I said, pushing him away. "My way."

I forced a confident smile as I undressed him: taking off his jacket, unbuttoning his shirt, revealing his massive chest. *Don't let your fingers shake, Cynthia.* The pearls couldn't help me with my nervousness. Though earlier spells had helped me pursue other erotic adventures, I'd never been with a man as beautiful as this.

At last he was bare-chested, a magnificent animal of muscle and heat. I unzipped his pants and slid them down his hard thighs. And there was his cock, thick and long and curving to the right, aching just for me.

He grabbed my hand and curled it around his shaft. So dominant, so demanding.

I pulled my hand back and slapped him lightly across his mouth. "What did I tell you? One more move and I'll leave."

He grunted impatiently and reached for my breasts.

"That's it." I pushed him into a chair.

"What are you doing?"

"Tying you up and gagging you. That'll teach you to obey."

He looked gorgeous bound to the chair with his own silk ties, his muscular chest and hard thighs flexed to attention. His cock stood up in invitation. I wanted nothing more than to sink down on his hard shaft and kiss him, running my fingers through his black curls, as I had dreamt a thousand times a day.

At the same time, I couldn't stop thinking of all those nights at work when he had strode right past me, frowning and talking on his cell phone. I needed to make him ache for me. Beg for me.

I found his phone in his pants. I stood behind him and slipped out of my dress, until I stood only in my heels and the pearls. He could hear the slithering of the fabric and made noises of protest through his gag, trying futilely to turn his chair so he could see me naked.

"Patience, my sweet." I caressed his silky hair.

I opened his phone. The first photo I took with it was of the under curve of my breasts. I leaned over his shoulder and showed. "What do you think? Do you want to see more?"

He made eager noises of affirmation. I stepped back and took a photo of my ass, a bit difficult to do, and showed him that, then followed with one of my nipples. With every photo I showed him, more and more eagerness oozed from his rock-hard cock. Finally I snapped a picture between my legs and showed him that, eliciting a groan of heartfelt anguish through his gag. I ruffled his hair and looked down at that beautiful cock, straining so hard and upright. I could have ridden him right there. But I wasn't done teasing him yet.

I removed the gag. "Please," he said hoarsely. I continued untying him—everything but his hands.

He rose awkwardly from the chair with his hands still tied behind his back, and came at me with that massive chest, those hard legs, that determination firing his eyes. "Now," he demanded. "No more games."

But I merely laughed and ducked into the shadows of his bedroom, as he helplessly tried to pin me against the walls. I was too slippery for him and dodged beneath his arm, laughing as he cursed. He pinned me against the closet door and thrust his cock between my legs, beginning to groan with relief. But I escaped again—and a second later, felt myself falling onto the bed. He'd hooked one impatient leg around mine, throwing me off balance.

He fell on top of me and squirmed deliciously on my breasts, my stomach, yanking his hands against the silk binds. But I'd tied him well. "Damn you!" he cursed in that same dominant voice I'd heard echoing through the corridors at work so many times. My pussy gave a wet throb of longing and at last I rolled him over and straddled him, groping for a condom in his bedside stand.

His cock filled me like a long-awaited promise, so thick I gasped. He laughed and moved his hips beneath me, enticing me with every thrust. I rode him slowly at first, then faster, adjusting to his size until I was coming down on him in a rapid rhythm, howling as my blood filled with fire. I couldn't stand it anymore; I wanted to feel those massive hands on my bare skin. So I untied them.

In a flash, he had me pinned to the bed, his fingers roaming over my body. "You're mine now," he grunted, driving his cock into me, "and I'll never let you go."

I arched my back, moaning as he fucked me faster and harder, the rutting beast I'd always dreamed he'd be. He was gritting his teeth, fucking me so fiercely than the bed was shaking, slamming into the wall. My pussy was a molten crucible of heat, my clit thrumming with excitement.

"Fuck me from behind," I begged. This was how I'd fantasized him fucking me so many times. Obligingly he flipped me onto all fours and drove into me again, this time winding my long hair in his fist and yanking it, just enough, as if I were simply an animal he was going to fuck and control and own. Helplessly I began to come, my pussy throbbing over and over around his cock, until he gave a long pained groan and shuddered behind me.

He fell back into the sheets, wet and exhausted. "Incredible," was all he muttered.

I glanced at his nightstand clock. It was after three AM. I couldn't risk staying much longer.

Suddenly he reared up. "One more picture," he demanded. "This time of all of you."

Why not? It wasn't really my face or body he might share with friends or strangers. I sprawled back on the pillows and opened my legs with a confident smile.

And then he tossed his phone aside and crawled into the sheets next to me, one heavy arm of possession slung over my chest. He was asleep in no time. I knew I should leave but I stayed anyhow, watching his eyelashes on his cheek, his rumpled hair. *Don't fall in love, Cynthia.* This was only a night. My pearls seemed to shift with the reminder to protect my heart from this cocky, swaggering man. I tried not to think about how hard it would be to work near him again—to watch those beautiful lips, that gorgeous smile, while he'd never know it was me he'd shared this night with.

Still my heart gave a little pang when I looked outside and saw the gray light creeping over his garden. Daybreak was almost here. I slipped out of bed and looked for the last time at his sleeping naked body. Then I picked up my gown from the floor.

It had lost its shimmer. It was already reverting back to a polyester slip. I felt my breasts; they no longer filled my hands. My body was changing back to its original shape. I went into his closet and found a soft T-shirt, a coat that hung to my knees, and stole out of his magnificent house.

I left the slip on the floor of his bedroom. A souvenir of the night he was mastered by a woman he would never see again.

That night a driving winter rain coursed down my cottage windows. I thought of the beach, and the ashes of my spell washing out to the ocean. I lit three black candles and burned an incense of mugwort and sandalwood as thanks to my ocean sisters for their gifts. Then I curled up on the window seat and leaned my cheek against the glass, telling myself that it was best that Justin never know it was me, the office cleaning girl, who had loved him so forcefully.

The knock on the door took me by surprise.

Justin stood on the cottage steps. His black hair clung wet to his high cheekbones in the rain. He held up his cell phone and showed me the photos of that naked girl who'd commanded his cock last night—not the voluptuous chestnut-haired beauty, but the thinner, mouse-haired me.

"I may not understand how you did it," he said, "but I'm still not letting go of you."

He stalked into my humble cottage. His expensive coat dripped on the wooden floorboards as those intelligent green eyes explored my rooms, taking in my altar of candlesticks and smoking incense.

"A witch," he said. "I've heard the rumors about your family. I never believed them."

"Everyone underestimates me," I said. "That's their mistake."

Then he spied the black pearls gleaming in the candlelight on my altar.

"You wore those last night," he said.

My heart began to race as he slipped the black pearls over his head. I half expected them to shatter at this betrayal. Instead they betrayed me by gleaming beautifully from his sculpted chest.

Our eyes met. And he walked toward my bed.

I watched helplessly as he peeled off his wet clothes, confident in his masculine nakedness. There was no spell or trick to help me now as he turned to me with that confident smile and rudely stripped off my slip until I was naked. Then he tied my hands behind my back.

"You're mine now, aren't you?" he said, walking over to the bed. He patted it in a gesture for me to obey. "My slave tonight, to dominate and control."

I wanted to tell him it wasn't true. That the pearls only obeyed my whims. But the truth was that I'd always been his to command, and now he knew it. And so my bare feet traveled to him, spellbound by lust or sorcery or the silent urgings of the ocean spirits who gathered in the room tonight, urging me to succumb to the biggest spell of all and give myself in love.

RED AND THE BIG BAD WOLF

Poetic Desires

Red didn't want to be tamed, quieted or cooed to. Much like the horses she loved to ride, her spirit begged to be free, dash away from the responsibilities of her life and gallivant as she wished all day and night.

Red wasn't named Red because of her hair, though her rich brown betrayed hints of the color under the brilliant light of the autumn sun. Nor was she named because of her lips, plump and full, brighter than any others, only pink when she was sick.

No, Red was named after her character, and her unyielding temper. From the start she wanted her way always, turning red hot with rage when she didn't get it, and storming through anyone in her path who would defy her.

Red's parents saw her strength, her resilience, her determination all as assets for her future life as queen. Still, they worried. Who could calm their wild child? Who would be able to reason with her, talk to her? Who could tame her fury, be a partner to her while also wearing a crown?

Her teachers tried to tame Red with varying degrees of success. Red was brilliant, they all agreed, but it was her innate intelligence, not reasoned study, which locked in her knowledge.

Her riding instructor saw how Red connected with the wild mares and hoped that by taming them she would find peace as well. Not even this worked. As Red broke her horses, it seemed she absorbed their lost spirit, firing herself up anew.

Finally Red's parents went to the only other person they could trust, a person powerful enough to calm even their hotheaded daughter—the Grandmother of the forest.

Her home was deep inside the trees. Most lost their way before ever finding her. It was known she had cast spells to stave off the unwanted, to confuse those with ill intent toward her and outright reject anyone who sought to hurt her.

She lived alone, though not really. The trees, the plants and the animals were her constant companions, telling her the secrets of the land. Everyone loved and feared the Grandmother of the forest, and for good reason.

Before an envoy from the palace knocked on the Grandmother's door, she had already heard of his approach in whispers from the moss and weeds and the chatter of birds passing by. When she opened her cabin door, she greeted the scared young man, barely beyond boyhood, with a smile.

"I come as messenger from her and his majesties, the rulers of a realm, Queen Alisa and King Ryan, begging for your assistance."

"And what would these monarchs wish of me?"

"Their daughter, the princess heir, her grace Red is, well..."

"Unruly, undisciplined, intelligent beyond measure but more stubborn than twenty mules."

The messenger's face was aghast.

"News cuts through even the thickness of the woods, young man. I know of her. What would these rulers have me do?"

"They ask for your assistance in teaching her."

"You mean taming her."

Grandmother turned back inside her home and walked toward the kettle boiling over her fire.

"She is to be queen, oh wise mage, but who will she listen to? How will she lead, when all her actions are born of impulse? Who would marry her? Rule with her? Work to keep the peace of the dual kingdoms?"

"What you ask I can do, but it will have its price."

Grandmother saw her reflection in the dark brew bubbling. Saw how the years had been kind to her, even in her extended age. There were rewards to power, to the gift of magic, however subtle they may be.

"The queen and king will pay anything, give you anything."

"Yes, boy, that is assured. I meant the price they will have to accept, what they will have to endure, for their daughter, the princess, to be tamed. And the man who would do it, the man who would be their new king. I will require no payment for this task, for they will pay in other ways."

"The queen and king wish only for their daughter to rule with an even hand and calm heart beside a devoted man who would help guide and assist their daughter to do so."

"Very well."

Grandmother pulled a handful of herbs from her cloak pocket and cast them into the brew. As the shards of leaves fell, kissing the surface of the liquid, she saw him, and her, and the future that lay ahead for the land.

"Inform the queen and king that they must send their daughter into the forest to seek me. Tell the girl she is to visit me to honor the crown's promise to the land. Tell her she must find me within a day, but give her no provisions. She has some skill in archery. Allow her a bow and ten arrows. Then set her off and make it known that no one from our realm is to give her assistance. No one."

"Yes, mage. I will send notice to the monarchs at once."

"Envoy, remember my warning. Give them that message first. By accepting my help, they accept whatever consequences befall hereafter."

He crept up to the cabin with light steps, careful of every footfall. No one underestimated the magic of the mage. No one had come this close to culling the Grandmother of the forest. But no one was as skilled as the Big Bad Wolf.

He liked the name the other hunters had given him. It fit his frame and his personality. Gave him a reputation that spread throughout not just the dual realms but many lands beyond. So when the man arrived seeking him, only him, for a specific job, he knew he had to live up to his title.

But the Grandmother of the forest was something altogether different than anything he had ever accepted before. Wolfe had taken his fair share of life, always men who deserved their fates. Magic, though, had never been a part of his life. Only stories told to him by his mother before she passed from the pox. Now he sought to end the greatest magic in the dual realms. He sought to kill the mage.

Wolfe had heard stories of her cabin, heard how difficult it was to find. How people lost themselves in the forest. Lost their minds trying to find her. He would not let money bring him to such an end.

He gave his patron a simple counteroffer: one week. If he could not find her in one week, he would return his payment in full and be on his way. Magic was nothing he coveted.

So when he stepped into the forest and instinctively knew the way. When his steps felt less like tracking and more like a guided path. When he crept through the trees yet felt all eyes on him, Wolfe knew this would not be a normal kill. Within two days, he was at her front door. Glimpsed her through the window. His knife at the ready when he knocked.

When his hand met the wood, the door pushed open. She stood, her back to him, attending a brew over a fire.

"Sit, Wolfe. You are not going to kill me today."

Magic. It could be no other. He put his knife away and took a spot at the small table to the right of the woman, draping his heavy cloak across the back of the chair.

"How did you know I was coming?"

"They call me the Grandmother of the forest. How do you think?"

The eyes that had been on him. All manner of life had watched his journey to this cabin.

"You were sent to kill me. No need to tell me who. I already know. In fact, I know who hired them. It's an interesting story, one you don't need to know. Not yet, at least. What you will want to learn, though, is who you will meet today."

"And who will that be, mage?"

"The woman you will fall in love with and marry."

"I am not the marrying kind, Grandmother, no matter the woman."

"Doubt me, if you wish, but she is made for you and you for her. Once you set eyes upon her, you will know."

"This is a trick, I presume, a way to save your old life."

"No, it is a way to save us all."

The woman finally turned to him, holding a bowl of her brew.

"Soup, to comfort you from your long journey."

"What kind of enchantment is in this stock?"

Grandmother sighed, then took a sip.

"See, nothing to harm you."

Wolfe took the bowl from her and drank all the warm soup down. He did not realize how hungry he had been.

"More please."

"Of course."

As soon as he handed the bowl back, his eye lids felt heavy. As did his limbs. And the entirety of his body. And before he could react with anger or astonishment, he was asleep.

When Wolfe awoke, he felt cold. Damp. His eyes opened to view shafts of light piercing through the canopy of the forest.

He sat up. He recognized this section of the woods, far away from his seat at Grandmother's table. He no longer had his cloak or his dagger.

"Trickster woman."

"Excuse me?"

Wolfe jumped up and turned. As he held a stone in his hand, teeth clenched, ready for a fight, he saw her.

Her hair flowed luxuriously down to her waist, auburn with flashes of red. Her brown eyes matched her hair. Her red lips were plump, begging to always be kissed. She sat atop her horse, having somehow silently approached. Her red cloak was tied at her neck but thrown over her shoulders. Her hood was back. She was the most beautiful woman he had ever seen.

"I? Who are you?"

"I might ask the same of the man holding a weapon up against me."

"Wolfe. The name's Wolfe."

"Red. Are you lost, Wolfe?"

"Hardly." He threw the rock down. "Just on my way to visit a friend. Someone I need to have a little chat with."

"On foot? With the forest this thick?"

"I manage fine enough. Though, if the lady is offering a ride?"

"To a scoundrel who, for all I know, will steal my mare as soon as I let my guard down."

"Lady, as you might have noticed, I am without a weapon or a cloak. You have a bow and arrows, not to mention a horse and the high ground. If you think I might harm you, strike me down now. Otherwise, you help me and I'll help you."

"How do you suppose I need help?"

"Your arrows are dirty. A few are splintered. You tried to hunt for food, which means you've been out here for a while. Your lips, as beautiful as they are, are dry. You're thirsty, which means your water has run out. You need my help as much as I need yours."

Wolfe could see the thoughts turning in Red's mind, whether to trust a man she had just met. He could also hear her hungry belly's response.

"I'm looking for the Grandmother of the forest. Do you know where her cabin is?"

"She is, in fact, the friend I wish to find. I will help you hunt and then we both will have our visits."

Wolfe reached his arm up to Red. She reached down her gloved hand and helped hoist the man onto her mare.

"Which way?"

Wolfe stopped, thought. No, he felt the path he'd been entrusted with earlier. An awareness rushed over him. The magic that initially led him to Grandmother resumed in his mind.

"Go left. Follow the crooked stream to start."

Red sent her mare into motion. The horse bounded over the rocky ground and down toward the water.

With each movement of the horse, Wolfe felt Red's body against his. Her back against his chest. Her ass against his crotch. He placed his hands on her hips and squeezed, holding on tight to her body. He bent his head down and allowed the scent of her hair to fill him.

Had the mage been right? His anger for the woman seemed subdued as the Wolfe yearned to lose himself inside of Red.

Red rode fast.

"Why are you in such a hurry?"

"I am late. I was to find the mage two days ago, but I couldn't make out the way. My parents sent me on this quest, and I bring shame to them with my failure."

"Many men have lost their way in the woods. You are not the first."

"I am to learn from her, yet the way does not reveal itself. Does she not want me?"

"I do not know the ways of magic. But you have not lost your mind or your life. And you found me, who knows the way. I think that bodes well for your cause."

"You said you could help me hunt. We need to do that soon. I haven't eaten in a few days and can only keep this pace up if I find food."

"Stop the mare. We'll do it now."

"But all the noise I've made from the riding."

"Stop the mare!"

Red pulled up, shocked by Wolfe's command. Shocked that anyone would dare yell at her. But then she remembered—she had yet to tell him who she was. She liked not being treated as the princess. Liked being viewed as a person. She would keep up the charade a little longer. Maybe he would be the first to match her resolve.

Wolfe dropped down and assisted Red off her mare. Red tied

the reins to a nearby tree limb. She pulled her bow and arrows off of the saddle and joined Wolfe by the stream.

"What am I—?"

"Quiet."

"I have my bow."

"Quiet, woman." Wolfe turned to Red, his eyes at first annoyed but then melting into passion. "Are you always this stubborn?"

She looked at him for a moment.

"Well?"

"You told me to be quiet."

Wolfe's anger flared, and then turned to glee. He held his mouth to silence his laughter.

"You need to be quiet, calm if you are to hunt. Make your voice as soft as the bubbling brook. Make your movements as soft as a leaf falling to the forest floor. Step closer to me."

He waved his hand toward the front of his body. Red stepped lightly over the ground and stood in front of him. Wolfe placed his hands on her hips and turned her around. He spoke with his lips next to her ear.

"You must still your body, still your mind, like the stillness of the land around you. Hear the things your constant motions drown out. Hear the noise of nature. Listen."

Red listened, really listened.

"I hear."

Wolfe grabbed her hand and rested his arm against hers.

"Show me."

Red pointed as she spoke, her eyes closed.

"The water from the stream. The rustling leaves above us."

"Good. What else?"

"The birds flying across. The rabbit in the grass over there. The deer nibbling on the leaves."

"Good. Now pick up your bow. String an arrow. Aim for the deer."

Red opened her eyes and saw the animal about fifty yards away. Wolfe remained at her ear as she strung her arrow and eyed her target.

"Breathe. Slow. See where you want your arrow to land. And when you are ready. Release."

Her arrow flew from her hands, its path true, and struck the deer dead.

Red jumped up, and then turned and hugged Wolfe. She encircled her arms around the big man, her bow still in her grasp. As he eased into her embrace, she looked up at him. Looked up into his eyes. Saw the rich inner life they revealed. Saw the chiseled chin. The slightly crooked nose. And found herself awash in a feeling all over her body. Red wanted to reach up and kiss him. And she tried, but he turned his face away.

"The deer," said Wolfe.

"Yes, the deer."

The two of them made their way over to the carcass, started a fire, roasted the meat and partook of it before resuming their ride toward Grandmother's cabin.

Now, with each motion of the mare, both Red and Wolfe felt the other's body. Felt each brush. Each touch. Each jostle. The closer the two got to the cabin, the more restless they both became.

Wolfe still felt the magic of the path, felt the draw to the old woman's home. They came upon the cabin at nightfall.

This time, when Wolfe knocked on the door and it drifted open, the old woman was not inside. Instead, sitting on the small table right where Wolfe had been earlier, there was a note.

My dear Red,

I hope you find my cabin soon. I fear for your welfare in the forest. Who knows what or who you may come across? I shall return in the morning with you hopefully resting in my bed and ready to begin your lessons.

Grandmother.

"No mention of you."

"My visit was supposed to be a surprise."

"It seems she left us some soup."

"All yours. The deer filled me fine."

Wolfe watched as Red ate her fill and, unlike him before, did not fall asleep.

Wolfe stoked the embers under the kettle, lifted the pot away to make room and built a fire for himself and Red. He sat on the floor and warmed his body by the flames. Red sat next to him enjoying the heat.

Wolfe could think of nothing else but the way her body had felt against his as they rode. How much he wanted her. How much he never wanted to be without her. And he wondered if she felt the same.

Wolfe had wanted to kiss her when her mouth moved toward his. Had wanted to melt himself into her. But it would not have been true, for Wolfe wanted all of her, and he didn't know if she was willing to give that.

Wolfe shivered from the chill of the night. Even with the doors and windows closed, and the fire before them, the mage's home was still cold.

"Here." Red untied her cloak and tried to share it with Wolfe.

He was so big, though, it barely covered half his back.

"Thank you, Lady, but it will not do that way."

"Well, let's try this."

Red parted Wolfe's legs and nestled herself inside of his lap. She draped her cloak around his back, just barely covering his frame, pulled his arms around her chest, and lay back into his body.

Wolfe could not take it any longer. She was next to him, so close to him, her body against his, her heat. And her lips so close to his.

Wolfe pinched her chin and turned her head toward his. He wanted to kiss her, ravish her, take her. But he loved her. He knew it to be true. He loved her.

"If you do not leave. If you do not now push me out of this cabin and bar the door and windows, I will take you. All of you. Until I am sweaty and exhausted. Until the sun comes through the glass and shines on our writhing bodies. I want you, need you, Red. All of you. And if you do not feel as I do, tell me now while I still have the power to stop myself, while I still have the power to love you more than my desire to be inside you."

"Wolfe."

He saw again as her mind worked. Instead of waiting for her reply, he spoke.

"Bend your will to me, my Red, and I will not break your heart."

That was what she truly wanted, what she truly craved. Never before had Red known someone who drove her so, who twisted up parts inside her being she never knew existed. The unleashed ferocity of her soul yearned for this man. Even as she craved to break free, a part of herself, a part of her being she didn't know existed, felt pulled to do whatever he wished, whenever he wished it, however he wished it.

"Kiss me. Take me. Ravish me. Love me."

She moved her lips toward his. He pulled away again. Wolfe saw the sadness in her eyes, but this was not how he wanted her. Throwing his hands back, he dashed her cloak to the floor. Standing, he looked down on her beautiful face.

"Beg."

How could she want this? How could she desire this from anyone? And yet, a spark ignited in her being.

"Please, my Wolfe. My body needs to be taken by you. I want to please you, to be loved by you, to be tamed by you."

His arms pulled her up toward him. He ripped open her shirt. Went for her neck. Bit hard. She gasped, pain and pleasure mixing in a way she never knew possible.

He grabbed her hair. Pulled her face to his. Partook of her lips. Pulled off her shirt. Pulled down her pants. Wrenched off the fabric with her boots.

He scooped her up in his arms. Her body naked, shimmering in the firelight. She felt alive like never before.

Wolfe walked, found the mage's bed. Threw Red onto it. Pulled out his cock. Shoved Red's mouth onto it. Tangled his fingers in her hair. Bent over and bit her ass. She yelped as she took all of him into her throat. She gagged, and felt not humiliation as she had expected but affection, adoration, love. She wanted to be taken by this man. Wanted to be fully his, to be owned.

Wolfe pulled her mouth off his cock. Flung her back onto the bed. Climbed on top of her. Held her wrists down. Glided his cock against her lower lips.

"Ask me. Beg me. Let me know you want this as much as I want you."

"I want you, my Wolfe. I need you inside me. Having me in whatever way you wish. My body wants only to please you. My body needs your touch. Take me. Ravish me. Love me."

He entered her without hands. She gasped. And whimpered. And cried out her pleasure at being his.

He nibbled her breast. Sucked on her nipples. Entered her over and over again. She cried from her ecstasy. Cried from having this man inside of her. Cried at finally letting go, letting another be in control, and loving every moment of it. She had found a place, a home, she had never known existed. A pleasure and a peace only this man had ever given her. She wept at the revelation.

He ravished her until the sun came up, light streaming on their sweaty exhausted bodies, hair and limbs tangled. Love made flesh in them.

"Do you believe me now, Wolfe?"

Wolfe's eyes shot open. The mage sat in a rocking chair across from the bed, knitting needles in her hands, a square of fabric being shaped.

Red's face nestled on Wolfe's chest, his arms still around her. He felt her breath on his skin.

"What is going on, Grandmother? Why was I sent to kill you? How did I end up back in the forest? Why did she find me? Why do I feel so for her and she for me? Why did last night happen? It feels as if it was all a dream, and yet I am here and she is beside me."

"I think part of that is obvious. She is beautiful. You are handsome. But the rest is more complicated."

"Tell me."

"We live in a land divided by two realms separated by the deep dark forest. Most dare not to travel between the realms, through the forest, for the way is less than safe. But those that do see what is possible, the land that could be conquered by either if the other so chose.

"The forest, the land, wants to be united, but not by war. That is man's way.

"Magic made her who she is and you who you are. Magic bore her hot tempered, Red as the fire that burns inside her. Magic bore you strong, strong enough to tame her, strong enough for her to want your taming, strong enough to help her in what lies ahead.

"She is the Princess Red, heir to throne of one kingdom. You are the bastard son of the other monarchy. Together you will unite our land without the destruction of the forest, without war's abundance of death."

"Grandmother, I don't understand."

"She didn't find you. You found her. The soup you drank had but one purpose: to send you to the place of your love. And so you were sent to her."

"And when she drank, she didn't disappear. She stayed with me. She loves me. But how are we to unite the land? How are we to make the dual realms one?"

"You need not worry about that. Just love her. Love her, guide her, honor and protect her, and the magic will do the rest."

THE LAST DUCHESS

Kristina Wright

Esmeralda's eyelids fluttered open and, for a moment, she had no idea where she was. Her head hurt fiercely and her mouth was parched. She could hear the rustle of fabric as she shifted and felt the weight of one of her heavier gowns. A duchess's royal finery and the smell of...earth. Death. Blood. Fear coursed through her and her lips parted to call out for her husband, Duke Graylin of Fairmore. Then her memory came flooding back. The beatings that began as playful and amorous and became increasingly violent, the horror of overhearing her husband's intentions to dispose of her, the frantic scramble to secure her escape, and, ultimately, the deep sleep that facilitated her release from evil.

It had seemed an impossible task, escaping her husband. Had she simply disappeared into the woods around the great manor, he would have questioned—and tortured—every last man, woman and child of the surrounding villages to determine her location and bring about her return. She couldn't ask that of anyone. Death was the only true means of escape, and faking her death had been the only true method of saving her life. The duke meant to kill her and replace her with a younger wife, one whose dowry would net him the waterways around their lands and secure favor with the king. A wife who would endure his beatings silently and stoically as Esmeralda had, until her eventual demise from a fall down the stone steps of the grand hall—the end Esmeralda's husband had been planning for her.

The duke was not only cruel, he was shrewd. A man, no matter how highborn, couldn't simply kill off his wife in cold blood without the people rising up in protest. But accidents happen and the duke was a true master of accidents—after all, more than one of his detractors had died in a hunting accident, or drowned in his own bathwater after a night of debauchery. And then there was the first duchess... Esmeralda's predecessor was said to have hung herself upon the eve of their fifth wedding anniversary when she had failed to give the Duke an heir. Esmeralda wondered at the truth in that story.

The duke was a brilliant man, but the duchess was smart and had been raised to think for herself. Finding someone who loathed the duke as much as she did wasn't hard—finding one who would assist her proved more difficult. But Esmeralda had her own power, her own strengths—and a small fortune squirreled far away from the duke's reach. The wizard who now stood before her would have everything his heart desired if she were able to escape her husband.

"Ah, so you've awoken," he said, his rough voice soothing in the darkness.

"How—how long was I asleep?" she asked, saying the words carefully, her throat as rough-sounding as that of her savior.

"It has been a fortnight, milady."

"The duke—" A shudder slipped up her spine, at the memory of his cruel face twisted above her. "The funeral?"

"The duke believes you dead. The funeral was held three days past," the wizard said. "Your body, as it were, was placed on display in the main hall. You were delivered to my care by your trusted servants, their pockets heavy with your gold, while a coffin laden with stones was placed in the family plot."

"No one guessed?" Esmeralda dared feel a spark of hope. "No one questioned my sudden death?"

There was movement from the wizard, the shaking of his head in the depths of the gloom. "Many wept over you, a few whispered of the duke's cruelty and treachery."

"But none raised a sword against him," the Duchess claimed wearily. "None would defend my honor or my life."

A lantern flared to life on the table beside her and the wizard's face came into view, lined and scowling beneath his heavy hood. "Seek your own revenge, Duchess. Do not fear a man who would seek to kill you."

"I don't want revenge."

The wizard's eyes narrowed. "What is it you do want, Duchess?"

Esmeralda's rubbed her eyes wearily. "I only want to live free and happily."

What Esme didn't say, what she couldn't bear to tell the wizard, was that she wanted to live happily with the man the duke had promised to be, strong and capable, loving and masterful. In fact, there had been a time when she welcomed the click of the cuffs and the kiss of the cat-o'-nine-tails because such sweet torture led to the greatest of pleasures when accompanied by amorous attentions. She had thought, falsely so, that she had found the man of her dreams. But the duke had proven to be only a cruel sadist, aroused by her pain and disinterested in her pleasure. Her life had been risked for dark desires masked as love. No more. Never again.

"I want only to be happy and free," she said again, keeping those secret passions to herself.

But she suspected the wizard was wise and knew the truth.

Time passed and the duchess kept to herself, using her gold to secure a small cottage deep in the woods and far from the clutches of the duke and his cronies. The wizard had been kind, despite his rather gruff nature, and sent his apprentice George along every fortnight with provisions. She had been raised by practical parents and despite a sketchy royal lineage, she was still able to care for her own needs, tend her own garden, chop wood for the winter and survive.

And yet...she sometimes longed to do more than simply survive. Her heart was filled with a need to love and her body longed to give and receive pleasure. Even after all she had endured at the hands of the duke, Esme often woke from fevered dreams, clutching her bed linens and craving both pleasure and pain.

One morning, after she'd had a particularly vivid night of dreams, George arrived on her doorstep with a parcel of provisions from the wizard.

"'Allo, Esmeralda," he called as she met him at the door. He had dispensed with formal titles, at her insistence. She could never be called Duchess again, of course, and "Lady Esmeralda" hardly seemed fitting given her new life.

"Good morning, George! I hope you are well!"

She was almost giddy with excitement, as George was likely the only person she would see for at least another fortnight, with the exception of the occasional traveler who might see the smoke from her fire burning and stop to inquire about a meal.

"I am, I am, milady," he said, though his expression and

formality suggested otherwise. "I've brought you news of the duke."

For a moment, Esme's heart froze in her chest. Surely he didn't know she was alive. Surely, after nearly a year, she was safe from his abuse.

"Yes?" she asked, terrified to hear the words he would speak.

"He's dead."

Whatever she expected to feel, it hadn't been grief. And yet, something inside her seized. "What? How?"

"It was a duel, milady. Over you."

"What? Me? Why? He believes—believed—I was dead."

George shook his head sadly. "One of your servants turned. The duke, it seems, had your grave exhumed and found only rocks. Under threat of death, one of your ladies fled for her homeland and the other—" He shook his head again.

Esme was reeling at this new turn of events. She reached blindly for a chair and lowered herself into it. "Why on earth would he want to dig up my body?"

The wizard's apprentice scowled. "Dark magic, Esme. He intended to use your bones to conjure, as he claimed, 'the perfect ladywhore.'"

Esmeralda shuddered. The duke had gotten worse. "How? Who killed him?" she asked, barely a whisper, already knowing the response.

"The wizard."

And so it was. The duke was dead, the duchess was free. Because of the wizard.

"What of the wizard now, George?"

The apprentice shifted his gaze. "He is in hiding."

"Thank goodness for his magic," Esme murmured.

George tilted his head and opened his mouth to speak, then shook his head. He began unloading parcels from his bag. "In any case, the wizard said to tell you he will be by to see you soon. Until then, he hoped you would enjoy a few things."

From his bag, amidst the sack of potatoes and a bundle of spices, came the sound of a cat mewing. George retrieved the animal, wrapped in a bit of shimmery rose-colored cloth, and presented it to her.

"A gift from the wizard," he said. "He thought you might be lonely."

The cat, a medium-sized ginger tom, looked at her with green eyes as she took his weight against her bosom. "I am lonely," she murmured softly. Then, as George bid farewell and left her to her own devices, she added, "In ways no cat shall ever be able to satisfy. Certainly not this one."

But she was grateful to the wizard. Grateful for the gift of food, the cat companion and for giving her peace of mind. She needn't confine her days to living in the woods. She could go back into society now.

And yet...that didn't feel quite right. She had let the wizard do for her what she couldn't do for herself. She felt a coward. The duke had been evil and rather than spare the next duchess the agony of abuse, she had run. She felt ashamed.

The cat meowed and she put down a saucer of cream to appease him. "Oh dear cat, what have I done?"

The cat cocked his head quizzically, reminiscent of the way George had looked at her. Then he lapped at his milk.

Esme went about her daily chores, her mind distracted. By the time she crawled into her bed that night, she was heartsick. Not over the duke, but over what she had not done. Did the man deserve to die? She thought perhaps he did, but still...it pained her to think of him, so she cast him out of her mind and fell into a deep sleep.

And she dreamed.

* * *

The wizard came to her in her dream, his cloak swirling about him like a cloud. He was an ominous presence, towering over her and scowling.

"What is it you want, Duchess?" he asked, leaning toward her until they were nose to nose. "What do you want?"

She closed her eyes to his knowing, green-eyed stare. "I just want to be free," she cried. "I told you that!"

"And yet, you are sad."

She shook her head, though the words were true.

"You are brokenhearted over the duke's death. Your soul is adrift. You are lonely."

Again, she shook her head. She could feel his anger like a palpable touch.

"Do not lie to me, girl!"

Even in her dream she could feel his power. "No!" she cried. "It's not him I miss!"

"What then?"

"Companionship," she said. "I'm lonely."

The wizard laughed. "Companionship? You have a cat now. You can move to a town. You don't need companionship. The duke didn't offer you that. What is it you miss, if not him?"

Even in her dream state, she was loath to say. She turned away from him, hid her face in her hands, embarrassed. Shy. Humiliated. And, strangely aroused.

"His touch," she whispered. "No! Not *his* touch, but a man's touch. A man's caress."

The wizard didn't laugh at her confession, nor did he chide her for being a foolish woman. He only said, "What else?"

"Other...things," she admitted. "Less gentle."

"Hard?"

She nodded, meeting the wizard's knowing gaze. "Rough."

He nodded in time with her. "Rough. Tell me."

She didn't want to speak, but she had no choice. "I wish to be bound. Tied, held down. Unable to escape."

"He did that?"

She nodded. "Yes, but—while I liked what he did, I did not like him. He was cruel. What I wanted, craved, was love and passion with the pain. He had only pain to offer. I took what he gave until I could no longer bear it. Until the threat of death seemed far too great a punishment for the crime of enjoying pain."

He watched her. "You want the pain to be pleasurable."

She nodded.

"You want to be fucked."

She hesitated only a moment before she nodded again.

"Pleasure and pain. You shall have it, my duchess, if that is what you desire."

"It is," she said, her darkest longings in those two words.

She awoke suddenly, almost violently, sitting upright in bed. Her skin felt feverish and she feared for a moment she was ill. But no, the fever emanated from between her thighs, making her skin tingle. She wrenched herself free of the bed linens, tugging up the hem of her nightgown in order to cool herself. The cat sat at the end of the bed, unperturbed, staring at her with his green, unblinking eyes.

Green eyes much like those of the wizard of her dream. Did the wizard truly have green eyes? She couldn't recall. She could barely remember what he looked like, in fact. Hadn't he been old? Hunched? She remembered the gloom of his keep and a cloak pulled down over his head, further shadowing him from her gaze. Oh, and white hair. It was white, wasn't it? Wizard's magic, she realized. Changing his appearance so she could not incriminate him.

"Dear girl, if you spend all your time wondering what I look like, we'll never resolve anything."

She blinked. Once, twice. But the cat only yawned.

"I'm still dreaming," she murmured, kicking at the cat. "That must be it."

The cat yelped—a very human yelp—and jumped to a high shelf. "Wench, keep that up and I'll thrash you." Despite his words, there was humor in his voice.

"Who are you?" she asked, already knowing the answer.

"Would you like to see?"

She didn't know what she wanted, other than a cure for this damnable heat that had overtaken her. She nodded.

The cat jumped from the shelf and perched on the end of the bed once again. And then he changed. *Flowed* was the word that came to mind. His fur seemed to shift and expand as the feline grew to fill the end of the bed. The fur faded to reveal skin, the skin shifted into human form. And then, in a matter of moments, the cat became a man.

"Thank the gods I'm sleeping, or I'd think I was mad," she mumbled.

The man cocked his head in an oddly familiar way, his green eyes staring through her. "Are you sleeping?"

She realized quite suddenly she was not. Had she ever been sleeping? She shook her head, unsure of anything except that there was a man—a very naked, handsome ginger-haired man—at the end of the bed.

"Don't recognize me without my usual garb?" he asked dryly, rising to stand beside the bed.

Esme averted her gaze, or attempted to, but it was difficult to ignore his body. His arousal. His magnificence. She had, of course, seen other naked men. The duke had been attractive, if cruel, and the handful of young men she had been with in all but the holy sense—were handsome each in his own way. But this man—her breath caught in her throat.

"No, Sir, I do not know you. I am quite certain we have never met," she said formally, not the least bit amused at the incongruity of her words and his nakedness.

In a move almost too quick for her eyes to see, he ripped the blanket from the end of her bed and tossed it in a flourish over his head. Tucking his chin to his chest and hunching his shoulders, he asked, "Now do you recognize me?"

And there, in the shadows of the folds of a blanket, with his face falsely lined by the way he held his head and his body bent in a deliberate attempt to minimize his height, was the wizard who had helped her escape the duke.

She scrambled on hands and feet to the other end of the bed. "What sorcery is this, Magician? What is your purpose here?"

He laughed, seemingly not at all disturbed by her indignation. "Oh, my dear duchess, there is no sorcery! Well, at least not in this," he amended. "I was a cat, yes. But I had to escape the duke's court somehow. As you can imagine, they are calling for my head over his death. But the rest—" he tossed the blanket to the floor. "You saw what you wanted to see. You needed me to be an old, impotent wizard whose intentions were pure. And so I was."

She absorbed this new knowledge, a growing feeling of need building in her as she stared at his beautiful form. Her fate had rested on his broad shoulders and now—now he stood naked in her cottage by her bed.

"You're staring, Duchess." His voice was rough with something like arousal but she could also hear his laughter.

"You're naked, Wizard," she said, finding her courage. "Why is that?"

He shrugged elegantly. "I can't take my clothes with me

when I shift forms."

She nodded slowly. "And…that?"

He had the decency to blush—a quite enchanting thing on a fair-haired man—as she gestured at his erection. "Ah, well, that was something I wanted to discuss with you."

"You wanted to discuss your hard cock with me?" His blushing had made her feel positively impertinent. "It's a lovely specimen, but it seems there would be better things to do with it than…discuss it."

He looked shocked. Delighted. A smile spread across his rugged face. "Ah, Duchess, I feared you would hate me for ending the life of your husband. I am sorry if I have caused you pain."

"You saved my life," she said. "You were brave where I was a coward. You did what I could not do. And in the process, you certainly saved others from a worse fate. You did nothing wrong, Wizard. Nothing."

"I did it for you, Duchess. You are not a coward and I am not brave. I simply did what needed to be done." He fell to his knees beside the bed and took her hands in his. "But thank you for this absolution."

"Thank you for giving me my freedom."

He studied her carefully. "Is there more I might give you?"

She moved to pull her hands from his grasp, but he held fast. She met his gaze steadily. "You heard what it is I miss. What I am lonely for."

He nodded slowly, caressing the backs of her hands with his thumbs. "I did. I also heard your fevered dreams during your deep sleep. You cried out many, many times."

"I did? What did I say?" she asked, and then wished she could reclaim the words as soon as they were spoken aloud.

"You begged to be punished," he said. "You cried out for the whip, asked to be bound. You told me in intimate detail what you wanted."

It was her turn to blush, but there was no escaping his steady green-eyed gaze. "Were you appalled? Did my words disgust you?" They were questions she didn't want to ask, but she had to. The duke had indulged her wickedness because of his own sadistic streak, but afterward...he would tell her what a dark soul she must possess to *enjoy* his punishments. She had wept tears of humiliation, fearing he was right. But now, staring into the eyes of the wizard who had saved her life and heard her confession, she felt strong.

"No, my dear heart," he said. "I was surprised at first, I will admit. But your words...they awoke something long dormant inside me. An answering desire. One that would surely complement your own. If you would allow me to show that side of myself to you."

She could not help herself. She was hungry with her desire and though he was simply too good to be true she felt something stir inside her. Desire, yes, but something else. She would not put a name on it, but she knew this man could be her match. In all ways.

"Show me," she said. It wasn't a dare—it was a willing, and exciting, relinquishment of control.

He stood, still holding her hands, and pulled her from the bed. "Hold on to the door frame, my duchess," he said, but there was an authority to his voice that hadn't been there a moment before. "And do not let go, no matter what I do to you."

She slipped her nightgown off one shoulder and then the other, letting it slide down her body and pool on the floor. Now she was as naked as he. She shivered at the promise of things to come. And then she obeyed, stretching up on her toes to wrap her fingers around the wide beam above the door. He didn't make her wait. The first touch was a gentle caress from her neck to the base of her spine. She shivered because it tickled and she opened her mouth to tell him so, but then he slapped her bottom hard and all that came out was a yelp. A second slap quickly followed the first, followed by a firm caress of the warmed skin.

"Is that what you crave?"

She nodded. "And more."

"More."

The doorway was big enough to allow him to walk around her. Cupping her chin in his hand, he stared into her eyes. "Whatever I do to you will be because you want it," he said. "Do you understand?"

She nodded, unable to speak.

"I will cause you pain, but it will be accompanied by exquisite pleasure. If there is no pleasure for you, then I will stop. You have only to say the word." "What word?"

"No."

She had expected an incantation, something magical or at least secretive. "No? That's all?"

He nodded. "That's all, Duchess. Say 'no' and I will stop. I will ask you if you mean it and if you say no again, I will stop."

She felt empty. "You will not touch me again?"

He must have heard the disappointment in her voice because he chuckled and tilted her face up to his. "I will not cause you pain if you tell me to stop. The rest, the pleasure, in whatever form you want it, will continue. Better?"

She nodded eagerly. "Oh yes."

"Good."

He kissed her then. She had stripped naked and presented herself before him without ever so much as kissing him. He wasn't her husband or even her betrothed. She marveled at her wantonness with a stranger.

A stranger who had saved her life, she reminded herself. A stranger who had killed the duke rather than allow him to hunt her down and kill her. A stranger who seemed to know her and wanted to give her what her heart desired. That was enough. She clutched at the door frame while she kissed him, obeying that one command to not let go even while she tried to convey with her mouth just how much she wanted him and how grateful she was that he had come to her.

"Ah, if you fuck like you kiss, you will be the death of me before the night is over," he said, his crude words arousing her. "I will have you, Duchess."

She looked down at his impressive erection. "And I will have you," she said, her confidence as strong as before even as she submitted. She was captivated by him, to be sure, but her body was growing impatient. Her ass felt hot from the smacks he had delivered there, and her nether regions had grown heavy with want. She needed him. Now. "I am yours," she said simply. "Take me."

He cupped her breasts in his hands, as if testing their weight. "You are very beautiful," he said. "I cannot wait to bind you to the bed."

"Why not now?"

He pinched her nipples hard enough to make her go even higher on her toes and lean away. She whimpered, but she did not let go of the door frame.

"To be honest, I like this for now. You are bound only by my words. You do not know me and cannot trust me, so I want you to be able to think only about what I am doing to you and not about how you might get away."

At that, he twisted her nipples and pulled them out from her breasts, forcing her to arch her back and press them into his hands to lessen the pain. She cried out, but she held fast to the frame.

"You like that?"

She was torn. Did she like it? It hurt like fire and her breasts throbbed with the agony of the twisting of her nipples. But she nodded, for she did like it. "I love it," she confessed. "It makes me feel alive."

He dealt a stinging slap to the side of each breast in turn. "Beautiful."

"More, Sir," she said. "Please. It's been a long, long time."

His cock literally twitched at her words, as if it had a mind of its own and was as eager as she was. The wizard reached down and stroked it once and her mouth watered to taste him.

"Indeed? Well then, since you are so eager…"

He moved behind her once more and she braced herself for another stinging slap, but he twisted her long hair around his fist and tugged, gently enough. "Let go and face the bed."

She did as he said, enjoying the tingling at her scalp as he yanked harder on her hair. "Yes, Sir."

"Good. Now bend over and put your hands on the bed, Duchess. And wait." He released her hair and stood behind her, waiting for her to comply.

Putting her hands on the bed was easy enough, but the waiting was excruciating. She could feel him studying her naked body and knew he was examining her, open and ready for him. She was embarrassed and aroused.

She was slipping away into another place, focusing on her breathing and distracted by the way her hair fell across her face and tickled her nose. And then he slapped her ass hard and she was fully in the moment, aware of his presence, his breath, the width and breadth of his hand falling on her tender backside again and again. She yelped and squirmed, but she kept her hands pressed to the bed and her head down, taking everything he gave her and wanting more.

"Ah, you're wet for it," he said. "I can see your arousal glistening on your pussy. You're dripping, my naughty duchess."

She was; she could see the wetness on her thighs, trickling from her as he gave her the pain she craved. The pain that twisted into pleasure and melted her insides. She felt his hand slip between her thighs, could see his large fingers parting her lips and sliding inside, first one, then two. She moaned as he stroked her, screamed when he withdrew his fingers and pinched her swollen clitoris. Bright sparks of pain flickered behind her closed eyelids and gave way to a climax that nearly buckled her knees.

He tsked with amusement. "I forgot to tell you to restrain yourself until I allowed your release, but I had no idea you were so easily brought to orgasm."

"I'm sorry, Sir," she gasped, though her true feelings were a mixture of joy and embarrassment.

"Don't be sorry. I love this new discovery. Oh, the things we will do," he said, directing his hand between her thighs and smacking her—there—on her wet pussy.

She cried out again, the intensity of her orgasm combined with the slight sting of the slap sending her spiraling into another spasm of pleasure. "Please, Sir, please," she moaned, arching her back to him. "Please."

"Please, what?"

"Fuck me, please, Sir," she said, repeating it again and again until he grasped the fiery cheeks of her bottom and spread her before him. Then, in one magnificent thrust, he was buried inside her to the root.

She cried out at the intensity of being suddenly filled after feeling so very empty, and clutched at the bedsheets as he drove himself into her again and again, administering slaps to her bottom, her thighs, the sides of her breasts, with each thrust.

"More," she cried. "Please, more!"

And he gave her more. He fucked her until her knees went out from under her and she lay with her upper body flat on the mattress and her knees pressed to the hard floor. He fucked her with his teeth pressed against her shoulder, nipping and scraping her fevered flesh. He grabbed her hair up into his hands once more, arching her neck back, kissing her and biting her while he pulled her hair and drove his cock into her.

Her screams filled the room and she was so lost in this moment with this man it wouldn't have mattered if the entire court burst in on them then. She would have this man—and he would have her—and nothing, not the dead duke, the scandal that shrouded her death, the wizard's peculiar magic or the whispers of her own conscience that she was a wicked, wicked girl would stop her from having what she wanted.

Again, she climaxed, loud and lustily, slipping farther off the bed as the sheet in her grasp slid across the mattress. The walls of her pussy clenched around him, and she felt his release as he groaned with his mouth pressed to the side of her neck. She was lost, was her first thought. But then she realized the truth. She had been found.

"That was magnificent, Duchess" he said after a time, cradling her sweat-slickened body against his chest.

She laughed, feeling free in body and soul. "Stop calling me that. I am Esmeralda. But I do not know your name."

"Aleck, but it has been a long, long time since anyone called me anything but Wizard. The duke paid quite handsomely for my services and threatened my family if I failed him."

"Family? You have a wife?" she asked, startled—and suddenly very sad.

He squeezed her hands. "No. My parents are alive, and I have two sisters who have husbands and children of their own. And I would not—could not—risk anything happening to any of them. And so I served the duke. Until now."

"What will you do?"

He ducked his head, almost bashfully, which made her feel tender toward him. "I can make my magic anywhere, milady. I thought, perhaps, you and I—"

"You want to stay with me?"

He nodded. "We could go to another village together. Travel. See the world beyond the villages we both know."

She considered it. She did not know him at all, but it somehow felt right. "I think I would like that."

He cleared his throat. "Do you think you might, someday, feel more than desire for me?"

"More than this?" She laughed again, gesturing at their entangled bodies.

"Yes. More." And then he said the word. "Love."

She watched him carefully, her heart thumping in her chest. Dare she take a chance on another man? One who was capable of magic? "Do you think you might love me?"

He held her tight. "I have loved you since the first moment I set eyes on you at court. You are strong and self-assured, educated and kind. And so very beautiful," he said. "And you are as passionate about life as you are about fulfilling your desires. Yes, dear Esmeralda, I think I might love you. I already do."

It was all she needed. "Then let's see the world, my darling wizard. I don't think magic will be required for me to find happiness in your arms. Only time and your love and more of your very special magic."

"You shall have all your heart desires, my dear. Always."

ABOUT THE AUTHORS

VALERIE ALEXANDER lives in Arizona. Her work has been previously published in *Best of Best Women's Erotica, Best Bondage Erotica, Best Lesbian Erotica* and other anthologies.

MICHELLE AUGELLO-PAGE (michelleaugellopage.wordpress.com) writes erotica, poetry and dark fiction. Her work has appeared in art galleries, audio and e-book formats, online and in print journals and anthologies. Her fairy-tale erotica has been published in *Fairy Tale Lust* and *Lustfully Ever After.*

LAILA BLAKE is a bilingual German native with an MA in applied linguistics, working as a writer and translator in Cologne. She spends her days listening to folk music and penning character-driven romance and erotica. Her debut novel is *By the Light of the Moon.*

VICTORIA BLISSE (victoriablisse.co.uk) is equally at home behind a laptop or cooker and loves to create stories and baked goods that make people happy. Passion, love and laughter fill her works, just as they fill her busy life.

ELIZABETH BROOKS (EveryWorldNeedsLove.blogspot.com) lives in Virginia, where she masquerades as an uptight corporate cog by day while publishing smutty stories by night. When she's not writing or editing, she loves reading, role-playing games, photography and geeky gadgets.

BENJAMIN CREEK is a law student and an ardent aficionado of fairy tales and classic science fiction. He lives in Virginia with a loved and fabulous wife and an also-loved but slightly less fabulous lizard.

ROSE DE FER's writing often explores themes of bondage, D/s, petplay and paranormal romance. Her stories appear in *Red Velvet & Absinthe* and numerous HarperCollins Mischief anthologies including *Underworlds*, *Submission* and *Forever Bound*. She lives in England.

POETIC DESIRES (thatsmessedupblog.blogspot.com) is a writer who has been exploring kink since she graduated from college in 2005. She has been active in the East Coast kink community for the past three years.

KANNAN FENG (kannanfeng.wordpress.com) lives in a century-old building by an inland sea. Her current interests include tektites, juggling, pastry and invertebrates. She has also written the novellas *Lord of Misrule, Charming Monsters* and *Under the Skin*.

A Kiwi-Brit hybrid, **JANE GILBERT** has an accent that confuses her friends, her neighbors and her children. She blogs about kink and writes erotica from behind her very chintzy curtains in rural England.

ARIEL GRAHAM is a Reno native who is happiest surrounded by sagebrush and sunshine. She shares her home with her husband and a pack of felines. Ariel's work has appeared in *Best Lesbian Romance*; *Please, Sir* and *Please, Ma'am* and in online magazines like Oysters & Chocolate and Clean Sheets.

TAHIRA IQBAL (tahiraiqbal.com) is a multi-published writer who discovered that by adding tension to erotica, you get more bang for your buck. You can find her work in various Cleis Press anthologies and on digital platforms.

MICHAEL M. JONES is a writer, reviewer and editor. He lives in Southwest Virginia with too many books, just enough cats and one extraordinarily understanding wife. His stories have appeared in numerous anthologies including *Lustfully Ever After* and *She-Shifters*, and he is the editor of *Like A Cunning Plan: Erotic Trickster Tales.*

CATHERINE PAULSSEN's (catherinepaulssen.com) stories have appeared in *Best Lesbian Romance 2012* and *2013*, *Girl Fever*, *Duty and Desire*, Silver Publishing's *Dreaming of a White Christmas* series and in anthologies by Ravenous Romance and Constable & Robinson.

L. C. SPOERING (lcspoering.wordpress.com) is a native of Denver where she lives with her husband, two kids and too many pets. Her work centers around the human experience, relationships and the lives lived in between. She has appeared in several erotica anthologies and is working on selling her first novel.

KATHLEEN TUDOR (KathleenTudor.com) is an author and editor, with stories in anthologies from Cleis, Circlet, Storm Moon, HarperCollins Mischief, Circlet, Xcite and more. Check her stories out in *Kiss Me at Midnight* and the anthologies *Take Me* and *My Boyfriend's Boyfriends.*

After years in the corporate world, **CATHY YARDLEY** (cathyyardley.com) now writes urban fantasy and romance, and celebrates her freedom from the cube farm in an undisclosed location somewhere near Seattle. She is the author of the fairy-tale erotic romances *Crave*, *Ravish* and *Enslave.*

ABOUT THE EDITOR

Described by The Romance Reader as "a budding force to be reckoned with," **KRISTINA WRIGHT** (kristinawright.com) is the editor of over a dozen published and forthcoming Cleis Press anthologies, including the best-selling *Fairy Tale Lust: Erotic Fantasies for Women*. Other titles include: *Dream Lover: Paranormal Tales of Erotic Romance*; *Steamlust: Steampunk Erotic Romance*; *Lustfully Ever After: Fairy Tale Erotic Romance*; *Duty and Desire: Military Erotic Romance*, *xoxo: Sweet and Sexy Romance* and the *Best Erotic Romance* series. She is also the author/editor of the cross-genre *Bedded Bliss: A Couple's Guide to Lust Ever After* for Cleis Press and the author of the erotic romance *Seduce Me Tonight* for HarperCollins Mischief. Her fiction has been published in over one hundred anthologies and her nonfiction has appeared in numerous publications, both print and online. She holds degrees in English and humanities and has taught composition and world mythology at the college level. Originally from South Florida, Kristina is living happily ever after in Virginia with her husband, Jay, and their two little boys.

More from Kristina Wright

Best Erotic Romance
Edited by Kristina Wright

This year's collection is the debut of a new series! "Kristina is a phenomenal writer...she has the enviable ability to tell a story and simultaneously excite her readers." —Erotica Readers and Writers Association

ISBN 978-1-57344-751-5 $14.95

Steamlust
Steampunk Erotic Romance
Edited by Kristina Wright

"Turn the page with me and step into the new worlds...where airships rule the skies, where romance and intellect are valued over money and social status, where lovers boldly discover each other's bodies, minds and hearts." —from the foreword by Meljean Brook

ISBN 978-1-57344-721-8 $14.95

Dream Lover
Paranormal Tales of Erotic Romance
Edited by Kristina Wright

Supernaturally sensual and captivating, the stories in *Dream Lover* will fill you with a craving that defies the rules of life, death and gravity. "...A choice of paranormal seduction for every reader. All are original and entertaining." —*Romantic Times*

ISBN 978-1-57344-655-6 $14.95

Fairy Tale Lust
Erotic Fantasies for Women
Edited by Kristina Wright

Award-winning novelist and erotica writer Kristina Wright goes over the river and through the woods to find the sexiest fairy tales ever written. "Deliciously sexy action to make your heart beat faster." —Angela Knight, the *New York Times* bestselling author of *Guardian*

ISBN 978-1-57344-397-5 $14.95

Lustfully Ever After
Fairy Tale Erotic Romance
Edited by Kristina Wright

Even grown-ups need bedtime stories, and this delightful collection of fairy tales will lead you down a magical path into forbidden romance and erotic love. The authors of *Lustfully Ever After* know your heart's most wicked and secret desires.

ISBN 978-1-57344-787-4 $14.95

*** Free book of equal or lesser value. Shipping and applicable sales tax extra.**
Cleis Press • (800) 780-2279 • orders@cleispress.com
www.cleispress.com

Happy Endings Forever And Ever

Dark Secret Love
A Story of Submission
By Alison Tyler

Inspired by her own BDSM exploits and private diaries, Alison Tyler draws on twenty-five years of penning sultry stories to create a scorchingly hot work of fiction, a memoir-inspired novel with reality at its core. A modern-day *Story of O*, a *9 1/2 Weeks*-style journey fueled by lust, longing and the search for true love.
ISBN 978-1-57344-956-4 $16.95

High-Octane Heroes
Erotic Romance for Women
Edited by Delilah Devlin

One glance and your heart will melt—these chiseled, brave men will ignite your fantasies with their courage and charisma. Award-winning romance writer Delilah Devlin has gathered stories of hunky, red-blooded guys who enter danger zones in the name of duty, honor, country and even love.
ISBN 978-1-57344-969-4 $15.95

Duty and Desire
Military Erotic Romance
Edited by Kristina Wright

The only thing stronger than the call of duty is the call of desire. *Duty and Desire* enlists a team of hot-blooded men and women from every branch of the military who serve their country and follow their hearts.
ISBN 978-1-57344-823-9 $15.95

Smokin' Hot Firemen
Erotic Romance Stories for Women
Edited by Delilah Devlin

Delilah delivers tales of these courageous men breaking down doors to steal readers' hearts! *Smokin' Hot Firemen* imagines the romantic possibilities of being held against a massively muscled chest by a man whose mission is to save lives and serve *every* need.
ISBN 978-1-57344-934-2 $15.95

Only You
Erotic Romance for Women
Edited by Rachel Kramer Bussel

Only You is full of tenderness, raw passion, love, longing and the many emotions that kindle true romance. The couples in *Only You* test the boundaries of their love to make their relationships stronger.
ISBN 978-1-57344-909-0 $15.95

*** Free book of equal or lesser value. Shipping and applicable sales tax extra.**
Cleis Press • (800) 780-2279 • orders@cleispress.com
www.cleispress.com